# ECHOES
# of
# EXISTENCE

Short Stories on Modern Realities & Life's Philosophy

BY RG SOMA

ISBN  979-8-89556-023-5

# Disclaimer

*The characters and events depicted in *Echoes of Existence* are entirely fictional. Any resemblance to actual persons, living or deceased, or real-life events is purely coincidental. The stories within this book are created solely for the purpose of exploring various themes and ideas, and they do not reflect or relate to any individual's personal experiences or life.*

# Contents

# Synopsis

Echoes of Existence: A Journey Through Life's Challenges and Philosophies offers readers a profound exploration of contemporary life, diving into the challenges, choices, and philosophies that shape our existence. This book is a reflective journey, with each chapter presenting a unique perspective on the struggles and triumphs that define the human experience.

The stories depict a thought-provoking exploration of the human experience, offering insights into the challenges we face in understanding ourselves and navigating a rapidly changing world. Each chapter serves as a reminder that, despite the darkness, there is always hope for change and redemption.

The book provides a deep and thoughtful exploration of the human condition, offering readers a multifaceted look at the challenges, choices, and enduring connections that shape our lives. Through these stories, the book invites reflection on our shared humanity and the resilience we find in the face of life's complexities.

This synopsis presents a cohesive and reflective exploration of the various human experiences and societal issues addressed in the book.

# About the Author

Soma Roy, known to readers as author RG Soma, hails from the vibrant city of Dhanbad in Jharkhand, celebrated for its prestigious IIT (ISM) and renowned as the Coal Capital of India. Having spent her formative years there, she completed her schooling before relocating to Kolkata for higher education. Soma achieved her BA (Hons) in English from the University of Calcutta and an MA in English from Rabindra Bharati University, an institution once graced by Nobel laureate Rabindranath Tagore.

In 2006, Soma moved to Singapore after her marriage, where she embarked on a diverse career that began with teaching and has now evolved into running her own startup as an HR Consultant. Her passion for writing, which ignited during her school days, was evident through her recognition for Hindi writing skills on Prem Chand Diwas. Soma has a remarkable ability to craft poetry and articles in both Hindi and English.

Her debut English book reflects her deep-rooted interest in exploring the multifaceted aspects of life, livelihood, and the challenges faced by a growing society. Through her writing, Soma aims to bridge connections and provide insight into the diverse experiences that shape our world.

# Acknowledgements

This book would not have been possible without the unwavering support and motivation from my Maa, Manas (hubby), Dadabhai & Mamoni- Bapi (in laws). Their constant belief in my abilities pushed me to act and bring this vision to life.

I extend my deepest gratitude to my English teachers (Kunalkanti Sinha Sir, Saumya Sengupta Sir) and English professors from Serampore College, who not only imparted knowledge but also instilled the confidence in me to express myself through words. Their guidance has been invaluable in shaping my abilities.

A special thanks to my son, Viraaj, whose insightful perspectives, along with those of his friends, on the current social matters greatly contributed to the depth of this work.

I am deeply thankful to my friends, whose constant support has been a steady source of strength. Your presence through every step of this journey means the world to me. Last but not least, this book is dedicated to my Baba (late father), whose blessings have made this possible.

Your encouragement and belief have made this book, Echoes of Existence, a reality.

# Chapter 1

# From Grey to Live

In life's beginnings often appear veiled in shades of grey, anticipating the vibrancy our priorities will bring. This journey turns the mundane into the extraordinary, with aspirations lighting the way to fulfilment. But what are these priorities that guide us through life's maze? Is it family, work, passion, or perhaps entertainment? Surprisingly, identifying these priorities is not as difficult as it seems. It comes down to perception, balancing necessity against desire, and ultimately, having enough to survive.

Shom, embodies the aspirations of the middle-class, with dreams of academic success and self-respect shaping her journey. Raised in a modest household, she learned the value of diligence and determination early on. As an above-average student, she excels academically, but her true essence lies in her multifaceted nature.

Despite her academic pursuits, Shom is a vibrant presence in her school community. She immerses herself in extracurricular activities with gusto, whether it's sports, elocution, music, or leadership roles. Her disciplined approach allows her to excel in these endeavours effortlessly. Unlike many of her peers, Shom doesn't need constant prodding from her parents to fulfil her responsibilities; she is self-motivated and driven by her innate desire to succeed.

However, beneath her studious facade lies a fascination with glitz, glamour, fashion, and makeup. From a young age, Shom has been drawn to the allure of the glamorous world, finding solace and joy in the transformative power of style. Despite her practical upbringing, she indulges in these interests, seeing them as a form of self-expression and a means to escape the monotony of everyday life.

Growing up in a place where the chasm between mere existence and truly living was starkly apparent, the concept of 'living life to the fullest' often felt like an elusive dream. Just beyond the threshold of Shom's home lay a slum area, where families eked out their livelihoods amidst the humdrum of daily struggles. Among them was their regular milk supplier, Bhuvan, who seemed content in the simplicity of his existence, tethered to his customers like us and his cherished cattle. Bhuvan's existence is defined by the relentless pursuit of survival. With three children to care for and a meagre income, Bhuvan finds himself trapped in a cycle of poverty and debt.

Unlike Shom, education is a luxury that Bhuvan cannot afford. The burden of loans taken to purchase his two cows, and one buffalo weighs heavily on his shoulders, forcing him to toil tirelessly as a milkman and a farm labourer to make ends meet. Despite his hardships, Bhuvan

is characterized by his unwavering honesty and integrity, qualities that have endeared him to Shom's family.

Despite their contrasting circumstances, Shom and Bhuvan share a deep bond forged by proximity and mutual respect. While Shom dreams of a future filled with academic achievements and glamour, Bhuvan's aspirations are anchored in the simple joys of providing for his family. Yet, amidst the differences that separate them, they find common ground in their humanity, reminding us that empathy and compassion transcend social divides.

Yet, despite their differing circumstances, their priorities intersected in unexpected ways.

For Shom, the pursuit of education held primacy. The word 'exam' resonated with an urgency that may have seemed alien to some, but for a middle -class family, it was the cornerstone of their aspirations. Shom, understood implicitly that the marks she garnered in those examinations held the key to unlocking the doors of opportunity, to sculpting a life beyond the confines of their current reality. But therein lay the question – to what end?

For Shom, the answer crystallized in a desire to become a teacher, to impart knowledge to Bhuvan's children and those of her neighbours who shared in her collective aspiration.

The aspirations of the community were remarkably homogeneous – a trifecta of professions: teacher, doctor, or engineer. It appears the collective consciousness couldn't fathom possibilities beyond these well-trodden paths.

One fine day, in the modest but cozy kitchen of Shom's family home, the aroma of freshly brewed chai wafted through the air. Sunlight streamed through the small window, casting a warm glow on the room's worn but well-loved furniture. Bhuvan, with a broad smile and eyes glistening with pride, shared the news of his accomplishment with Shom's mother. A sense of pride and admiration filled the room, mingling with the comforting scent of the chai. For Bhuvan, the payment for the newborn calf symbolized a significant milestone—a step closer to breaking free from the shackles of debt that had burdened him for so long. It was a moment of triumph, akin to Shom scoring well in her final exams. Despite the stark contrast in their pursuits— Bhuvan chasing life for survival, while Shom chases a life to live—the underlying theme of hope for a better tomorrow united them. Bhuvan's journey, though vastly different from Shom's, echoed the universal desire for progress and prosperity. It served as a poignant reminder that regardless of our circumstances, we all harbour dreams of transcending the limitations of our present reality.

For Shom, witnessing Bhuvan's triumph reignited her own sense of purpose and determination. It reinforced her belief in the transformative power of perseverance and hard work. As she reflected on Bhuvan's journey, she couldn't help but draw parallels to her own aspirations. Like Bhuvan, she too was chasing a brighter future—one filled with opportunities and possibilities.

In that moment of shared humanity, the lines between their worlds blurred, and the stark differences that once separated them faded into the background. What remained was a profound sense of connection—a recognition of the shared struggles and triumphs that define the human experience.

As they parted ways, each returning to their respective lives, they carried with them a renewed sense of hope. For in Bhuvan's victory, Shom found inspiration to continue pursuing her own dreams, knowing that despite the challenges that lay ahead, a better tomorrow was always within reach.

And so, they both held onto the belief that one day, the greyness of their existence would give way to a kaleidoscope of colors—a testament to the resilience of the human spirit and the unwavering pursuit of a life worth living.

Yet, amidst the rigidity of our predetermined destinies, there existed a glimmer of hope, a whisper of possibility. As we journeyed through the challenges the rigors of academia, we began to recognize the power of choice, the agency to shape our own narratives. While our initial priorities may have been influenced by societal expectations and pragmatic considerations, the seeds of individuality were quietly taking root within us.

In our lives, the transition from grey to vibrant hues was a gradual one, marked by moments of introspection and self-discovery. It was a journey of shedding the constraints of convention and embracing the boundless potential of our dreams. And as we embarked on this odyssey, we realized that our priorities were not static markers but ever-evolving guideposts, leading us towards a life truly worth living.

# Chapter 2

# The Weight of Hierarchy

In the chapter that follow, we will explore the myriad ways in which the weight of hierarchy manifests in society and corporate life, examining its impact on individuals and institutions alike. Through stories and insights from real-life experiences, we will delve into the complexities of power dynamics and the quest for equality in a world shaped by hierarchy.

As Tina entered the office for her first day, she took in her new surroundings with a mix of excitement and nervous anticipation. The open-plan workspace was bustling with activity, filled with the hum of conversation and the clatter of keyboards. Sunlight streamed through large windows, casting a warm glow on the modern decor.

Her new manager, Ms. Elyn, approached with a smile that didn't quite reach her eyes. The smile seemed more of a practiced gesture than a genuine welcome. "Hello, Tina. Welcome aboard," she said briskly. Instead of introducing Tina to her new colleagues, Ms. Elyn led her straight to a nearby meeting room. The door closed behind them, cutting off the lively sounds of the office.

The meeting room was stark and functional, with a long table, several chairs, and a whiteboard on one wall. Ms. Elyn handed Tina a stack of handbooks and began explaining the company policies in meticulous detail. She covered everything from office hours to email etiquette, her tone devoid of warmth or encouragement.

As Tina flipped through the pages, she noticed several odd rules interspersed among the standard policies. Ms. Elyn pointed out one in particular: "And remember, I have a severe allergy to polka-dot clothing, so please refrain from wearing anything with that pattern."

Tina blinked, momentarily taken aback. She nodded politely, though she couldn't help but feel a pang of unease. The introduction to her new job was not what she had expected. Instead of feeling welcomed and part of a team, she felt as though she were being briefed on a set of rigid protocols, some of which seemed more about personal quirks than professional standards.

The meeting ended as abruptly as it had begun. Ms. Elyn glanced at her watch and stood up. "That's all for now. I'll send someone to show you to your desk," she said, her smile reappearing, just as insincere as before. As Tina was escorted out of the meeting room, she couldn't shake the feeling that navigating her new workplace would be more challenging than she had anticipated.

For Tina, a newcomer to this world of corporate intrigue, the landscape is fraught with uncertainty and trepidation. As time goes by and Tina understands the complex terrain of office politics, she finds herself ensnared in the web of Ms Elyn's dominance—a predator stalking its prey with ruthless efficiency.

At the apex of this hierarchical pyramid sits Ms Elyn, a seasoned manager whose expertise and dedication have earned her the trust and respect of the company's CEO. From the humble beginnings of a startup to her current position of influence, she wields her authority with confidence, her every word carrying the weight of command. From the days when she was the sole employee of a fledgling startup to now, where her word carried weight in every decision, she had seen the company evolve and grow. But amidst the success, there lingered a shadow of unease—a reminder that power and privilege could breed toxicity if left unchecked.

From the start, Tina sensed a simmering tension between them—a clash of personalities and backgrounds that threatened to disrupt the delicate balance of the office dynamic.

As new employees joined the ranks, Ms Elyn found herself grappling with a sense of displacement. No longer the solitary figure she once was, she struggled to reconcile her position of authority with the need to foster a culture of inclusivity and fairness. Her close circle of allies provided solace, but even they couldn't shield her from the creeping feeling of isolation.

What began as subtle jabs and insinuations soon escalated into overt acts of hostility. From critiques of Tina's appearance to restrictions on her personal activities, Ms Elyn wielded her authority like a weapon, intent on maintaining her perceived superiority. Yet, beneath the veneer of confidence, Tina sensed a vulnerability—a fear born of personal struggles and insecurities. Despite Tina's best efforts to rise above the fray, the weight of Ms Elyn's scrutiny bore down on her, eroding her confidence and sapping her enthusiasm. With each passing day, she felt the walls closing in, the once vibrant office environment now suffocating in its toxicity. Yet, she remained silent, resigned to her fate in a system that offered no recourse for the marginalized.

But amidst the darkness, a glimmer of hope emerged—a realization that true strength lies not in power or privilege, but in resilience and self-respect. As Tina contemplated her future, she resolved to reclaim her agency, to defy the constraints of hierarchy and forge her own path forward.

For in a world where power and position reign supreme, it is those who dare to challenge the status quo who ultimately shape the course of history. And as Tina stood on the precipice of change, she knew that her journey was just beginning— a reflection of the indomitable spirit that resides within us all.

One fine day, Tina sat at her desk, the afternoon sunlight casting long shadows across the office floor.

The once-vibrant open-plan space now stood in quiet reflection of the disconnect she felt. Her fingers hovered over the keyboard as she composed her resignation letter, each keystroke a symbol of her liberation from the stifling environment that had consumed her for too long.

As she clicked "send," the weight of the decision began to lift. The email to her unempathetic boss, Ms. Elyn, was succinct but firm. Tina had reached her breaking point, unable to tolerate the toxic work culture and the relentless power plays that had come to define her daily experience. The office, which had once seemed like a place of potential and opportunity, now felt like a cage of indifference and manipulation.

When Ms. Elyn received the resignation email, her face remained expressionless, a stark contrast to the turmoil that Tina had endured. With an air of disinterest, she called Tina into her office. The room, bathed in harsh fluorescent light, felt colder than ever. Ms. Elyn's gaze was cool and detached as she reviewed the resignation letter, her eyes narrowing slightly but her demeanor unchanging.

Tina stood her ground, her voice steady despite the anxiety gnawing at her. "I've decided to resign," she said, her words clear and deliberate. "I believe I have a better opportunity elsewhere where my talents will be valued and where I can contribute more effectively."

Ms. Elyn offered a perfunctory nod, her response devoid of empathy. "Very well. We'll process your resignation. Please ensure you complete your tasks and hand over any pending work."

As Tina gathered her belongings, her colleagues watched with a mix of curiosity and sympathy, their expressions reflecting the strained atmosphere that had prevailed. The finality of her departure was both a relief and a bittersweet farewell to a chapter that had become increasingly disheartening.

Walking out of the office for the last time, Tina felt a profound sense of release. The oppressive weight of the toxic culture and the unempathetic boss was now behind her. The door closed with a soft click, marking the end of one era and the beginning of a new journey—one where she hoped to find a work environment that truly valued her contributions and respected her as an individual.

Moreover, hierarchy in corporate life is not limited to organizational structure alone. It extends to workplace culture, influencing everything from communication patterns and decision-making processes to opportunities for advancement and recognition. In environments where hierarchy is rigid and inflexible, individuals may find themselves constrained by the limitations of their rank, unable to fully realize their potential or contribute meaningfully to the organization.

# The Tug of War

In the intricate dance of relationships, the question of autonomy and freedom often comes to the forefront, particularly in the context of male dominance and its implications on a woman's right to make decisions regarding her own life and family.

Davis sat in his study, surrounded by the soft hum of machines and the glow of computer screens. For him, the world was a labyrinth of algorithms and data, a realm where logic reigned supreme. Raised as a single child, he had grown accustomed to solitude, finding solace in the silent companionship of robots and machines.

Opposite him, in the vibrant heart of their home, Lisa flitted from room to room, her laughter echoing through the halls. She was the embodiment of extroversion, her life a whirlwind of social gatherings and lively conversations. Married to Davis for a decade, their differences were as stark as night and day, yet their shared passion for music and exploration bound them together in a bonding of love and understanding.

Although Davis and Lisa were different in many ways, they shared a profound connection—one rooted in trust, friendship, and mutual respect. Davis, always the introvert, gave Lisa the freedom to chase her dreams, standing by her with steadfast support. However, beneath the surface, their relationship began to show signs of strain. While Lisa thrived in social settings, Davis stayed in the background, happy to let her take the spotlight. But as time went on, resentment quietly grew, fuelled by unspoken words and unmet expectations.

Lisa had always been the vibrant one in her relationship with Davis. While she thrived on social interactions and pursued her dreams with fervor, Davis, ever the introvert, quietly supported her from the shadows. Their relationship, built on trust and mutual respect, seemed unshakeable. However, as the years passed, the cracks in their bond began to show.

One evening, after a particularly heated argument about a trivial matter, Lisa sought solace in the company of her close friends. Over coffee, she shared her frustrations, revealing how Davis' expectations had started to weigh heavily on her. To her surprise, many of her friends echoed her sentiments. Despite being financially independent, they too felt stifled by the need to seek permission from their male partners for simple things like visiting their parents or allowing their children to spend time with their grandparents.

The conversation opened Lisa's eyes to a harsh reality: the expectation that women should defer to their male partners was not unique to her relationship. It was a common struggle, deeply rooted in societal norms that relegated women to a subordinate role, undermining their sense of autonomy and self-worth.

As the discussion deepened, the women talked about the unequal burden they bore in showing respect to their partner's parents, while the same courtesy was not always extended to their own families. They realized that this double standard was not just about respect; it was about power. The men in their lives often held greater authority in subtle ways,

influencing family decisions and interactions with extended family members. This imbalance left the women feeling obligated to maintain harmony, even at the cost of their own well-being.

For Lisa, this realization was both painful and empowering. She saw the parallel between her struggles and those of her friends, recognizing that the issue wasn't just personal—it was systemic. Yet, through the turmoil, a glimmer of hope emerged, Lisa understood that true freedom didn't lie in submission but in standing up for herself, reclaiming her agency, and asserting her right to autonomy. Returning home that night, Lisa felt a renewed sense of purpose. She knew that the journey ahead would be challenging, but she was ready to take the first step. As she stood on the brink of change, Lisa realized that her story was only just beginning—a reflection of the strength and resilience that had always been within her, waiting to be unleashed.

The next day, Lisa confronted Davis with an honesty that had been absent in their relationship for too long. She laid bare her frustrations, her need for equal respect, and her desire to be heard. Davis, taken aback, listened intently, realizing the depth of the issues they faced. The conversation was raw and difficult, but it marked a turning point. Davis agreed to work on their relationship, recognizing the importance of mutual respect and equality.

But as Lisa and Davis began to rebuild their relationship, a larger question loomed: Would Davis' willingness to change have a ripple effect? Could his transformation inspire Lisa's friends to demand the same respect and autonomy in their own relationships? Or would the deep-seated norms that governed their lives prove too difficult to overcome?

The climax of Lisa's journey raises critical questions for us all: Can one relationship truly set a precedent for change in a broader societal context? Will Davis' efforts to treat Lisa as an equal partner encourage other men to do the same? Or will Lisa's friends remain trapped in the same cycle of seeking permission and feeling subordinate?

Ladies like Lisa must open about their struggles. By sharing their experiences and refusing to accept the status quo, they can spark conversations that challenge entrenched norms. Lisa's story is a call to action—for women to reclaim their voices and for men to listen, reflect, and change. The question remains: Will this change spread, or will the silence of the past continue to stifle the voices of the present? The future of countless relationships may depend on the answer.

Chapter 4

# Embracing Motherhood

---

Gouri woke up to the sound of her alarm, her mind already buzzing with the myriad tasks that awaited her. As a single mother, her days were a whirlwind of responsibilities, balancing her demanding job with the needs of her child. But amidst the chaos, Gouri found solace in the unwavering love she shared with her son, a love that sustained her through life's ups and downs.

With a quick kiss on her sleeping child's foreheads, Gouri tiptoed out of the room, ready to face the challenges of the day. As she hurried through her morning routine, her mind raced with thoughts of deadlines and meetings, her identity as a dedicated professional intertwining seamlessly with her role as a mother.

Gouri looked back to the day when she sat in her university dorm room, her heart aflutter with anticipation as she awaited the arrival of her boyfriend, Arjo. They had been inseparable since they first met, their love story, was the envy of their friends and classmates. She watched him enter the room, she sensed a shift in the air—a tension that hung heavy between them.

As they sat down to talk, Gouri's stomach churned with nerves, her mind racing with a million questions. But before she could voice her concerns, Arjo dropped a bombshell that shattered her world into a million pieces—he wasn't ready for this, he said, his words cutting through her like a knife.

In that moment, Gouri's heart broke as she realized that the man she loved was not prepared to stand by her side as she embarked on the journey of motherhood. But amidst the pain and uncertainty, a flicker of determination ignited within her—a resolve to embrace motherhood on her own terms, regardless of the challenges that lay ahead.

Despite the whispers of societal judgment and the weight of expectations bearing down on her, Gouri knew in her heart that she was ready to become a mother. She had always dreamed of starting a family, of nurturing a life of her own, and she refused to let anyone else's opinion dictate her choices.

With a steely resolve, Gouri faced the world head-on, her firm determination a beacon of strength and courage. She embraced her pregnancy with a sense of awe and wonder, marvelling at the miracle growing within her, even as she was ready to tackle the hardship of single parenthood alone.

As her pregnancy progressed, Gouri found comfort in the support of her friends who rallied around her with love and encouragement. Unfortunately, her family was not supportive enough.

And when the time finally came for her to welcome her baby into the world, Gouri's heart swelled with a love so pure and unconditional that it took her breath away. As she cradled her newborn in her arms, she knew with certainty that she had made the right choice—that motherhood was her true calling, her greatest joy.

But through it all, Gouri remained steadfast in her belief that love conquers all. With each hug, each kiss, and each whispered word of encouragement, she poured her heart and soul into raising her baby, knowing that she will be her greatest legacy, her reason for being.

The road ahead was not without its challenges. As her daughter grew older, Gouri grappled with the fear of not being enough, of failing to meet her needs and expectations. She worried about the impact of her absence on her life, of the sacrifices she had to make in pursuit of a better future.

And as she drifted off to sleep, her heart full of love and gratitude, Gouri knew that no matter what tomorrow brought, she would face it with courage and determination, for she was a single mother—a warrior, a survivor, and above all, a loving mother.

In the end, Gouri's journey taught her that love knows no bounds—that it transcends societal norms and expectations, and that true strength lies in the courage to follow one's heart, no matter the obstacles that may arise. And as she looked into the eyes of her precious child, she knew that she was exactly where she was meant to be—in the embrace of motherhood, surrounded by love, and filled with hope for the future.

At work, Gouri was a force to be reckoned with—a dedicated Dean for her institution, a trusted colleague, and a pillar of strength for her team. Yet, beneath her confident exterior lay a woman confronting with the weight of single parenthood, juggling the demands of her career with the needs of her daughter.

Despite the countless challenges she faced, Gouri approached each day with determination and resilience. From school pickups and doctor's appointments to managing household chores and finances, she wore many hats with grace and poise. Yet, beneath the surface, the strain of single parenthood took its toll, leaving Gouri feeling exhausted and overwhelmed at times.

Amid Gouri's journey through single motherhood, there came a moment when the strain of obligations threatened to overwhelm her, leading her down a dark and treacherous path, Gouri found herself teetering on the edge of despair, her spirit battered and bruised by the relentless onslaught of life's challenges.

As the days stretched into weeks and the weeks into months, Gouri's resilience began to wane, her once indomitable spirit giving way to doubt and uncertainty.

Faced with mounting pressure and unrelenting stress, she took refuge in the deadening grasp of alcohol, hoping to drown out the chaos that raged within her.

Yet, the temporary reprieve offered by alcohol proved to be fleeting, as Gouri soon found herself ensnared in its suffocating grip. Days blurred into nights, and nights into days, as she descended further into the abyss of addiction, her world spiralling out of control with each passing moment.

In the darkness, a flicker of light emerged—a beacon of hope in the form of Gouri's friends and colleagues. Refusing to stand idly by as she succumbed to her demons, they recognized the strength and resilience that had always defined Gouri. With great support and compassion, they were determined to lift her out of the depths of despair. With gentle yet firm encouragement, they helped Gouri confront her addiction head-on, guiding her towards the path of recovery with love and understanding. They listened without judgment as she poured out her fears and insecurities, offering a shoulder to lean on and a hand to hold as she overcame the rocky terrain of sobriety.

Slowly but surely, Gouri began to find her footing once again, her inner strength rekindled by the staunch support of those who cared for her. Armed with newfound clarity and determination, she took tentative steps towards a brighter future, guided by the love and encouragement of her friends and colleagues. As the days passed by Gouri's journey through recovery exemplified the power of resilience and the transformative nature of human connection. Each day, she grew stronger and more determined, her spirit uplifted by the knowledge that she was not alone. She had a steadfast army of supporters by her side, ready to lift her up whenever she stumbled.

While there were moments of struggle, the sense of joy and triumph made it all worthwhile. Whether watching her daughter excel in school or celebrating small victories at work, Gouri drew strength from knowing she was providing for her family and shaping a better future for her child. Absolutely, failure is an inevitable part of life's journey, a universal experience that touches us all at some point.

However, for single parents like Gouri, the weight of failure can often feel more burdensome, as they face the challenges of raising a child alone while also managing the demands of work, finances, and personal well-being.

In the face of failure, Gouri found the courage to persevere, to pick herself up and dust herself off, knowing that her child depended on her for strength and support. Through the trials and tribulations of single parenthood, Gouri learned that failure was not a reflection of her worth as a mother, but rather a natural part of the human experience. She embraced her mistakes and shortcomings with grace and humility, knowing that they were simply stepping stones on the path to growth and self-discovery.

And as she journeyed through the ups and downs of life as a single parent, Gouri came to understand that true strength lies not in the absence of failure, but in the courage to face it head-on, with resilience and determination. In the end, it was her constant love for her child that sustained her through the darkest times, reminding her that no matter how daunting the challenges may seem, the bond between a mother and her child is a source of infinite strength and inspiration.

Chapter 5

# Finding Acceptance

---

Harry and Shawn had been inseparable since childhood, their friendship forged in the fires of shared adventures and mutual understanding. They laughed together, cried together, and faced life's challenges side by side, their bond unbreakable and true.

But as the years passed and adolescence gave way to adulthood, Shawn began to realize that his feelings for Harry were more than just friendship. He found himself drawn to Harry in a way that he couldn't explain, his heart fluttering at the mere sight of his best friend's smile.

On a bright day of summer sun dipped below the horizon, casting a warm, golden hue over the park where Shawn and Harry had spent countless afternoons. The joy of their laughter and companionship never wavered in their lives. Shawn's feelings began to shift in ways he hadn't anticipated.

They sat on their favourite bench, the one that overlooked the serene lake, its waters shimmering with the last light of day. Harry, as always, was animatedly recounting a story about his latest adventure, his eyes sparkling with enthusiasm. Shawn listened, a familiar, comforting sense of being home enveloping him. There was something new in Shawn's chest—a fluttering sensation he couldn't quite ignore.

As Harry laughed, his smile broad and genuine, Shawn's heart skipped a beat. The way Harry's eyes crinkled at the corners, the warmth of his laughter—it all seemed to amplify the emotions Shawn had been grappling with. He shifted in his seat, trying to focus on Harry's words, but his gaze kept drifting to the gentle curve of his friend's lips.

The evening air was filled with the scent of blooming jasmine, mingling with the earthy aroma of freshly cut grass. Shawn took a deep breath, trying to steady his racing thoughts. He realized that his feelings for Harry had evolved into something more profound than the comfortable friendship they had always shared. It was a realization that both excited and terrified him.

Harry paused mid-sentence, noticing Shawn's distracted demeanor. "Hey, you, okay?" he asked, a note of concern in his voice.

Shawn forced a smile, though his heart was pounding. "Yeah, just... thinking about stuff," he replied, his voice betraying a hint of hesitation.

Harry studied him for a moment before returning to his story, but Shawn's mind was miles away. He found himself caught in the complexity of his emotions, torn between the joy of his friend's presence and the fear of how to express the deeper feelings that had been growing inside him.

As the sky darkened and the first stars appeared, Shawn knew he couldn't continue to hide behind the façade of casual friendship. The feelings he had for Harry were more than just friendship—they were a deep, resonant chord that had been struck in the symphony of his heart. He realized that his heart fluttered at the mere sight of Harry's smile not because of the comfort of familiarity, but because of a profound affection he could no longer ignore.

The evening ended, and as they said their goodbyes, Shawn's thoughts were consumed by the uncertainty of what the future held. He knew he had to confront his feelings, but for now, he could only hope that when the time came, Harry would understand and maybe, just maybe, feel the same way.

But despite his best efforts to suppress his feelings, Shawn's depression deepened, threatening to consume him whole. He felt lost and alone, adrift in a sea of uncertainty and self-doubt, his once unshakeable confidence crumbling beneath the strain of his unrequited love.

It wasn't until Shawn hit rock bottom that he finally found the courage to confide in Harry, laying bare his heart and soul in a moment of vulnerability. To his surprise, Harry responded with compassion and understanding, his unconditional support a beacon of light in Shawn's darkest hour. Though Harry couldn't reciprocate Shawn's romantic feelings, he valued their friendship above all else, promising to stand by his side through thick and thin.

In the end, Shawn realized that true love wasn't always romantic—it was the bond of friendship that had sustained him through the darkest of times, the constant support of someone who accepted him for who he was, flaws and all. And as he and Harry stood side by side, facing the future with courage and hope, Shawn knew that their friendship was a treasure worth cherishing for a lifetime.

Shawn's journey through depression highlights the profound impact that societal norms and expectations can have on an individual's mental health and well-being. Despite growing acceptance of diverse identities and expressions, many individuals still face stigma and discrimination based on their sexual orientation or gender identity. For Shawn, the fear of rejection and the pressure to conform to societal norms burdened heavily on his shoulders, exacerbating feelings of shame, isolation, and self-doubt.

As Shawn wrestled with his feelings for Harry, he faced a barrage of negative messages from society—ranging from classmates who bullied him to the broader culture that often marginalizes LGBTQ+ individuals. These external pressures, coupled with internalized shame and self-criticism, created a toxic mix that eroded Shawn's sense of self-worth and left him feeling hopeless and alone.

Despite the support of his family and relatives, Shawn's struggles with depression were compounded by a lack of understanding and acceptance from those around him, particularly his peers. The relentless bullying and ostracization he experienced at school only served to deepen his sense of despair, reinforcing the belief that he was somehow unworthy of love and acceptance. In Shawn's case, depression became a coping mechanism—a way to numb the pain and escape the harsh realities of his daily life.

One evening, feeling overwhelmed by the weight of his internal and external battles, Shawn sat alone in the corner of his room. With a heavy heart, he closed his eyes and whispered a prayer for acceptance and understanding. As he spoke to the silence, he longed for a world where he could be seen for who he truly was and hoped for the strength to understand the pain he felt. But as his depression deepened, it became increasingly difficult for him to see a way out, to envision a future where he could be proud of his identity and live authentically.

Ultimately, Shawn's journey through depression underscores the importance of creating safe and supportive spaces where individuals can express themselves freely and openly without fear of judgment or discrimination. It also highlights the need for greater education and awareness around mental health issues, particularly within LGBTQ+ communities, where stigma and discrimination can exacerbate the risk of depression and other mental health disorders.

We can help create a world where everyone feels valued, supported, and empowered to embrace their true selves without fear or shame. For individuals like Shawn, that acceptance can serve as a lifeline, providing hope, healing, and the promise of a brighter future.

Chapter 6

# The Tragedy of Friendship

Jane was the heart and soul of the group, her infectious laughter and boundless optimism bringing joy to all who knew her. But beneath her cheerful exterior lay a deep-seated secret, one that she had carried with her for years, afraid of the repercussions it might bring if ever revealed.

As we unravel the layers of Jane's life, we uncover the deep bonds of friendship that tied her to her closest companions, each one carrying their own burdens and struggles. Together, they shared everything—or so they thought—until a shocking revelation threatened to tear their world apart.

Through Jane's story, we are confronted with the profound consequences of keeping secrets and the toll it can take on both individuals and relationships. As the truth slowly comes to light, we witness the devastating impact it has on Jane and those closest to her, as they cope with feelings of betrayal, guilt, and grief.

One afternoon, Jane sat in her cozy living room, chatting with her friend Chris. He looked both excited and anxious.

"Jane, I really appreciate this," Chris said, handing her a small box. "We're heading off on our honeymoon, and I need your help. Can you keep these things for me until I get back?"

"Of course, Chris," Jane replied with a reassuring smile. "It's no trouble at all. Have a fantastic honeymoon!"

"Thanks! Aaron will call you on this phone," Chris said, handing her a mobile phone. "He'll come by to pick up the box."

"No problem," Jane promised.

Months passed, and Chris returned from his honeymoon, brimming with gratitude. "Jane, you're a lifesaver! I totally forgot about this phone," he said, as they chatted about his trip.

"Glad to help!" Jane replied, handing him the phone. However, in the hustle and bustle, Chris forgot to take it back.

A few weeks later, Jane's world was shattered when a team of police officers arrived at her doorstep. "Jane Miller?" one officer asked, flashing her identification.

"Yes, that's me. What's going on?" Jane asked, her heart pounding.

"We need to talk about this phone," the officer said, sharing the numberwhich Chris had given her. "It's connected to a drug trafficking operation."

Jane's face went pale. "I had no idea. It was just given to me by a friend."

During the interrogation, Jane tried to explain. "I don't know anything about drugs, one of my friends gave me this phone to hold until his friend Aaron could come pick it up."

The officers continued to press. "Whose Aaron & Who is your friend?"

"I can't say," Jane insisted, "I really don't know about any illegal activity. I just did a favor for a friend."

As the investigation unfolded, Chris paid Jane a visit in the detention centre. "Jane, please don't mention my name," he pleaded. "I'm about to become a father. I need to protect my family."

"I don't know what to do, Chris," Jane said, her voice trembling. "I didn't know what I was carrying. But now, this is all falling apart."

"I swear, I didn't know about the drugs," Chris said earnestly. "I thought it was just some food items. I'll try to fix this."

Jane struggled with her conscience. "I can't keep your name a secret forever. But I can't ruin your life either."

Throughout the court proceedings, Jane maintained her stance. "The phone didn't belong to me; it was given to me by a friend," she said, refusing to elaborate further. The conflicting emotions of loyalty and self-preservation weighed heavily on her.

The trial concluded with Jane bearing the consequences of Chris's actions. Though Chris avoided legal repercussions, the burden of Jane's sacrifice haunted him. His conscience wrestled with the knowledge that his choices had led to the loss of a dear friend.

Jane's loved ones were left struggling with the betrayal. They saw Chris as complicit in her death, a painful reminder of broken trust. The shadow of Jane's sacrifice lingered over Chris' life, a haunting symbol of the profound impact of his choices.

In the end, Jane's story serves as a cautionary tale about the far-reaching consequences of secrets, loyalty, and the pursuit of personal gain at the expense of others. It highlights the critical issue of drug trafficking and its devastating impact, underscoring the importance of integrity, empathy, and the profound influence of one person's choices on those around them.

# Chapter 7

# Shadows of the Screen

In the digital age, where screens act as windows into alternate worlds, the shadows they cast can be darker than we dare to imagine. In the halls of Richard High School, nestled amidst the comforting embrace of academia, there existed a darkness that lurked just beyond the glowing screens of smartphones and laptops.

The situation in which Ryan faced cyberbullying began innocently enough, with whispers of gossip and rumours that spread like wildfire through the virtual corridors of social media. Among the targets of this digital vitriol was Ryan, a quiet boy with a gentle soul and a heart full of dreams. Behind the safety of their screens, his peers unleashed a barrage of cruelty, taunting and tormenting him with every keystroke.

At first, Ryan tried to shrug off the hurtful comments and malicious messages, hoping they would fade into the background noise of the online world. But as the cyberbullying persisted and intensified, he found himself increasingly isolated and vulnerable. The words cut deeper than any physical wound, gnawing at his self-esteem and eroding his sense of worth.

Day after day, Ryan logged onto his social media accounts with a sinking feeling in the pit of his stomach, bracing himself for the onslaught of hateful messages and hurtful remarks. Despite his attempts to avoid confrontation and maintain a semblance of normalcy, the relentless harassment followed him wherever he went, infiltrating every aspect of his digital existence.

As the cyberbullying took its toll on Ryan's mental and emotional well-being, he withdrew further into himself, retreating from social interactions and avoiding places where he might encounter his tormentors. His once-bright spirit dimmed under the weight of the constant negativity, leaving him feeling helpless and alone in a sea of hostility.

Then, one fateful night, as the darkness closed in around him, Ryan made a decision that would alter the course of his life forever. With trembling hands and tears streaming down his cheeks, he penned a final farewell to the world he could no longer bear to inhabit. And as he pressed send, the echoes of his despair reverberated through the silent void of cyberspace.

*Dear Friends,*

*As I sit down to write these words, my heart weighs heavy with sorrow and despair. For too long, I have carried the burden of pain and loneliness, suffocating beneath the battle of unspoken anguish and unshed tears.*

*You may wonder why I have chosen to take this drastic step, to end my life when there is still so much left undone and unsaid. The truth is, I can no longer bear the relentless torment of cyberbullying, the constant barrage of hatred and cruelty that has consumed my very soul.*

*For too long, I have tried to ignore the hurtful words and malicious taunts, hoping that they would fade into the background noise of the online world. But with each passing day, the darkness grew deeper, swallowing me whole and leaving me gasping for air in a sea of hostility and despair.*

*I want you to know that this decision was not made lightly, nor was it a cry for attention or sympathy. It is simply an acknowledgement of the unbearable pain that has plagued me for far too long, a desperate plea for release from the relentless torment of cyberbullying.*

*Dear Mum,*

*I am very sorry! I want you to remember me not for the way I died, but for the person I was – a son who loved and laughed and dreamed of a brighter tomorrow. I want you to cherish the memories we shared, the moments of joy and laughter that illuminated even the darkest of days.*

*Please know that I am at peace now, free from the shackles of suffering and despair. Though my time on this earth may have been brief, I hope that my story will serve as a reminder of the devastating consequences of cyberbullying and the urgent need for greater compassion, empathy, and understanding in our digital world.*

*Loving Ryan.*

The news of Ryan's death sent shockwaves through the community, shattering the illusion of safety and security that had once enveloped Richard High. His parents, grief-stricken and anguished, demanded answers from the school administration, desperate to understand how such a tragedy could have occurred under their watch.

As they sat across from the principal, their faces etched with pain and sorrow, they pleaded for accountability, for justice to be served in the wake of their son's senseless death. They demanded action to combat the scourge of cyberbullying that had claimed Ryan's life, to ensure that no other family would suffer the same unbearable loss.

But as the meeting ended and the promises of change rang hollow in their ears, Ryan's parents were left with a profound sense of emptiness. For no number of apologies or assurances could bring back their beloved son, nor could they erase the pain of his absence.

As they walked out of the school building, their hearts heavy with grief and their minds consumed by questions without answers, they vowed to honour Ryan's memory by fighting tirelessly to end the epidemic of cyberbullying that had robbed him of his future. And as they gazed up at the stars twinkling in the night sky, they whispered a silent prayer for peace, both for themselves and for all those who had been touched by the darkness of cyberbullying.

Cyberbullying, characterized using electronic communication to target and victimize individuals, knows no bounds, transcending geographical, cultural, and demographic barriers with alarming ease. From the comfort of their screens, perpetrators wield anonymity as a shield, unleashing a torrent of abuse upon their unsuspecting victims with impunity. The consequences of cyberbullying are far-reaching, extending beyond the digital realm to infiltrate every aspect of victims' lives.

In homes, schools, and communities around the world, the impact of cyberbullying reverberates with devastating consequences. Victims, stripped of their sense of safety and security, suffer profound emotional and psychological trauma, often leading to anxiety, depression, and even thoughts of self-harm or suicide. Families are torn apart as they fight with the anguish of seeing their loved ones suffer in silence, powerless to shield them from the relentless onslaught of online abuse.

But the ripple effects of cyberbullying extend beyond individual victims, casting a shadow over society. Communities fracture under the burden of division and distrust, as online interactions become battlegrounds for ideological warfare and identity-based discrimination. The erosion of empathy and compassion in the digital sphere threatens to erode the very foundations of social cohesion, leaving in its wake a fractured society devoid of solidarity and mutual respect.

Although Ryan's story ended in tragedy, his legacy lived on as a catalyst for change, inspiring others to take a stand against cyberbullying and to create a world where every individual is treated with dignity and respect. Through their collective efforts, the community of Richard High School emerged stronger and more united than ever before, proving that even in the face of darkness, there is always hope for a brighter tomorrow.

Chapter 8

# Unexpected Turmoil

---

Enrique and Laila had dreamed of their honeymoon in Istanbul for months. They had imagined wandering through the historic streets hand in hand, exploring the majestic mosques, and savouring the delicious cuisine. But fate had a different plan in store for them.

As they arrived in Istanbul, the city welcomed them with its vibrant energy and timeless beauty. They checked into a charming boutique hotel in the heart of the old city, excited to begin their adventure together. Their days were filled with wonder as they visited iconic landmarks like the Hagia Sophia and the Blue Mosque. They strolled through the bustling bazaars, marvelling at the array of spices, textiles, and treasures on display.

But as Enrique and Laila immersed themselves in the magic of their honeymoon, a dark cloud began to loom over their idyllic escape. The news was increasingly dominated by reports of escalating conflict between Israel and its neighbours, casting a shadow of unease over the region. Despite their attempts to remain focused on their love and the joys of their newlywed life, the growing tension was impossible to ignore.

One afternoon, as they were enjoying a leisurely boat ride along the Bosphorus, they received an urgent message from the hotel staff. The situation had worsened, and there were reports of unrest in the city. Authorities were advising tourists to exercise caution and stay indoors.

Enrique and Laila exchanged worried glances; their honeymoon paradise suddenly overshadowed by the spectre of conflict. Unsure of what to do, they made their way back to the hotel, their hearts heavy with concern.

As they huddled together in their room, the sound of distant sirens filled the air. Through the window, they could see smoke rising in the distance, a stark reminder of the violence unfolding just beyond their reach.

Hours turned into days as they waited anxiously for news and updates. The once bustling streets grew eerily quiet as fear gripped the city. Enrique and Laila clung to each other, finding solace in their love amidst the chaos.

Eventually, the worst of the violence subsided, and a fragile calm began to return to the city. With caution and relief, they emerged from their hotel. Their honeymoon had not gone as planned, but the ordeal had forged a deeper connection between them. As they walked hand in hand through the streets of Istanbul once more, they were profoundly aware of the strength of their love and their ability to face challenges together.

Enrique and Laila found themselves thrust into the heart of a tumultuous situation during what was supposed to be the happiest time of their lives. As the political crisis unfolded around them during their honeymoon in Istanbul, they were faced with a series of challenges that tested their resilience and strength as a couple.

In the face of escalating tensions, they remained calm and level-headed, prioritizing their safety while also seeking ways to help those in need. They volunteered at local shelters, offering comfort and support to displaced families who had

been affected by the violence. Their communication became their lifeline, as they talked through their fears and worries, providing reassurance and encouragement to one another. In moments of doubt, they leaned on each other for support, finding solace in their shared bond.

The global political crisis cast a wide shadow, affecting the lives and livelihoods of ordinary people like Enrique and Laila in profound ways. Initially, the crisis caused uncertainty and anxiety, disrupting their plans and injecting a sense of fear into their honeymoon experience. As tensions escalated, they found themselves grappling with the reality of being caught in a foreign city amidst turmoil, unsure of what the future held.

Practically, the crisis had immediate implications for their safety and well-being. They were forced to alter their itinerary, avoiding certain areas of the city and staying indoors for extended periods to minimize exposure to potential danger. This restriction curtailed their ability to fully enjoy the sights and experiences they had eagerly anticipated, adding a layer of disappointment to their honeymoon.

Beyond the immediate concerns for their safety, the political crisis had transformative effects that reverberated into their daily lives. Economic instability caused by the crisis led to fluctuations in currency exchange rates and increased prices for goods and services, impacting their budget and purchasing power. This strain on their finances added additional stress to an already tense situation, forcing them to carefully budget and prioritize their spending to make ends meet.

Moreover, the emotional toll of living through a political crisis cannot be understated. Enrique and Laila struggle with feelings of fear, uncertainty, and helplessness as they watched events unfold around them. They felt a sense of disconnection from their usual routines and comforts, as the crisis dominated their thoughts and conversations, overshadowing the joy of their honeymoon.

Despite the significant challenges the political crisis during their beautiful time, Enrique and Laila emerged with a deeper appreciation for the resilience of the human spirit and the sustaining power of love.

*In the crucible of life's relentless flow,*

*Where trials test the heart's enduring glow,*

*Enrique and Laila, in love's embrace,*

*Faced with adversity, stand face to face.*

*In Istanbul's ancient streets they tread,*

*Amidst turmoil where hope and fear are wed,*

*Their journey, a testament to love's decree,*

*As they confront the storm, resilient and free.*

# Chapter 9

# Unveiling Sheila's Hidden Garden

Sheila stood amidst a garden of talent, each bloom vibrant and distinct, while she felt like a humble bud yet to find its colour. Educated, articulate, and with a keen eye for aesthetics, she was the quintessential homemaker, her domain an exquisite tapestry of warmth and beauty. Amid her circle of friends, where careers and accomplishments bloomed like wildflowers, she often felt overshadowed, her own talents seemingly pale in comparison.

As she meticulously arranged the flowers she had picked from her garden, she couldn't shake off the nagging feeling of inadequacy. Her friend Lisa was a successful entrepreneur, her floral boutique renowned in the city for its exquisite arrangements. Another friend, Sarah, was a celebrated artist, her paintings adorning prestigious galleries. And then there was Sheila, content in her role as a homemaker, yet plagued by doubts about her own worth and talents.

Sheila had always loved home decor, effortlessly turning any space into a warm, inviting haven. No matter how many compliments she received, a nagging doubt lingered in her mind. Deep down, she felt as though she was just pretending to be creative, her work insignificant next to the accomplishments of her friends. What others saw as talent, she brushed off as mere hobbies, convinced that her efforts weren't deserving of real acknowledgment or praise.

One evening, as Sheila hosted a gathering of friends at her beautifully adorned home, she couldn't help but marvel at the effortless grace with which they started conversations about their careers and accomplishments. Lisa shared stories of her latest business ventures, Sarah enthralled everyone with tales of her upcoming art exhibition, while Sheila quietly listened, feeling increasingly like an outsider in her own circle.

As the evening wore on, Sheila's friend Diane, a perceptive soul with a gentle smile, pulled her aside for a private conversation. "Sheila," Diane began, her voice soft but firm, "I've known you for years, and I've always admired your talent for creating beauty in every corner of your home. Your eye for design, your attention to detail, it's truly remarkable."

Sheila's eyes widened in surprise, her heart fluttering with a mixture of disbelief and gratitude. "But Diane," she stammered, "what I do is nothing compared to what you and the others achieve in your careers. I'm just a homemaker, it's nothing special."

Diane shook her head gently, a knowing smile playing on her lips. "Sheila, don't sell yourself short. Being a homemaker is a talent, one that requires creativity, patience, and an firm dedication to creating a nurturing environment for your loved ones. Your passion for home decor isn't just a hobby, it's a gift, one that brings joy and beauty into the lives of everyone who enters your home."

As Diane's words sank in, Sheila felt a wave of realization wash over her. Perhaps she had been looking at her talents through the wrong lens all along, measuring herself against the wrong yardstick of success. Maybe being a homemaker wasn't just about cooking meals and keeping a tidy house;

maybe it was about creating a sanctuary, a haven of love and beauty where memories were made and cherished.

With newfound clarity, Sheila embraced her role as a homemaker with renewed confidence and pride. No longer would she compare herself to others or diminish her own talents. She was a gardener of the heart, tending to the seeds of love and beauty that bloomed within her home, each petal a proof to her unique and invaluable contribution to the world.

And as she looked around at her friends, she realized that each of them, in their own way, was a gardener too, cultivating their passions and talents with love and dedication. In the garden of life, there was room for every bloom, every colour, every fragrance, each one adding its own special magic to the canvas of existence.

As the evening ended, Sheila stood amidst her friends, her heart full and her spirit light. She may have started the evening feeling like a humble bud lost in a garden of talent, but now she knew that she was so much more. She was a flower in full bloom, radiant and vibrant, her true colors shining for all the world to see.

Indeed, Sheila's journey highlights a common struggle faced by many homemakers—underestimating their own talents and undervaluing the importance of their role. The societal perception of homemaking often fails to acknowledge the creativity, skill, and dedication required to create a warm and inviting home environment. Sheila's initial self-doubt reflects a broader cultural tendency to downplay the significance of homemaking compared to traditional career paths.

The issue extends beyond individual perception to systemic undervaluation. Homemakers often find themselves sidelined in conversations about achievement and success, their contributions deemed less worthy of recognition simply because they occur within the domestic sphere. This societal bias can lead to feelings of inadequacy and inferiority, as homemakers like Sheila internalize the message that their talents are somehow less valuable than those pursued in the professional world.

Moreover, the lack of external validation can exacerbate these feelings of self-doubt. Unlike individuals in traditional careers who receive performance evaluations, promotions, and awards, homemakers rarely receive tangible recognition

for their efforts. This absence of validation can reinforce the belief that their talents are insignificant or unworthy of acknowledgment.

Sheila's journey serves as a reminder that talent comes in many forms and that the value of one's contributions cannot be measured by societal standards alone. Whether in the boardroom or the living room, every individual has unique talents and strengths to offer, and it's essential to recognize and celebrate the diversity of skills that enrich our communities. By acknowledging and honouring the talents of homemakers like Sheila, we can create a more inclusive and equitable society where all contributions are valued and respected.

Sheila's story can be found in the words of the poet Rainer Maria Rilke:

"The only journey is the one within."

This quote speaks to the inner journey Sheila undertakes as she learns to appreciate her own talents and contributions, despite feeling overshadowed by the accomplishments of others. It reflects the internal realization and self-acceptance that she achieves, finding value and purpose in her role as a homemaker.

Chapter 10

## The Shifting Role

---

Rishabh adjusted the apron around his waist, feeling a sense of purpose as he stirred the simmering chicken curry. It was a typical afternoon in the Sharma's household, except for one significant detail – Rishabh was the one handling the domestic responsibilities while his wife, Sarah, was out working at her corporate job.

The decision to swap traditional gender roles hadn't been an easy one for Rishabh and Sarah. Growing up in a society where expectations were firmly ingrained, they initially faced scepticism and disapproval from their families and friends. But they discovered a newfound harmony in their relationship, through such change.

As Rishabh chopped vegetables with practiced ease, he reflected on the journey that had led them to this point. It had started with a simple conversation, a realization that their respective passions and strengths didn't align with society's preconceived notions of gender roles.

With Sarah excelling in her career in IT multinational company and Rishabh finding fulfilment in managing the household and caring for their two young children, they had made the bold decision to defy convention. It wasn't always easy – there were moments of doubt and insecurity, especially when faced with the judgment of others. But they had learned to tune out the noise and focus on what mattered most – their family's happiness and well-being.

As the aroma of the chicken curry filled the kitchen, Rishabh couldn't help but feel a sense of pride in the life they had built together. Their children, growing up in a household where gender equality was the norm, were thriving, unencumbered by outdated stereotypes.

But societal attitudes didn't change overnight, and they still encountered occasional resistance from those who couldn't understand or accept their choices. Yet, with each passing day, more and more families were challenging traditional gender norms, embracing a more equitable division of labour.

Rishab smiled as he heard the front door opening, signalling Sarah's return home from work. Stepping away from the stove, he wiped his hands on his apron and greeted her with a warm embrace.

"How was your day?" he asked, knowing full well the pressures and challenges she faced in the corporate world.

Sarah sighed, leaning into his embrace. "It was as busy as ever, but the aroma of the chicken curry you cooked up left me absolutely famished."

Together, they sat down to enjoy the meal that Rishabh had prepared, grateful for the journey that had brought them to this moment.

As Sarah and her daughter, Juhi, sat together at the dinner table, Juhi's innocent question hung in the air like a delicate mist.

"Mummy, why doesn't Daddy go to work like Serene's father does?" Juhi's curiosity sparkled in her eyes; her brow furrowed with genuine wonder.

Sarah paused, considering her response carefully. She smiled gently, reaching for Juhi's hand. "Well, sweetheart, everyone's family is different, and every family has its own way of doing things. Just like how we all have our favourite colors or foods, families have different ways of sharing responsibilities."

Juhi pondered this for a moment before nodding, her curiosity satisfied for the time being. But Rishabh, ever the poet at heart, felt compelled to add his own perspective.

Rising from his seat, he cleared his throat, his eyes twinkling with affection as he addressed his beloved daughter:

"In this grand dance of life, roles may differ, it's true,

Yet love and care, they never wane, they're constants, tried and true.

Your mom and I, we play our parts, in harmony we sway,

For in our hearts, we both know well, it matters not the way.

I toil not in an office tall, nor do I roam afar,

But here at home, I stand my post, beneath the guiding star.

For every task, both big and small, your happiness in sight,

Your mom and I, we stand as one, to make our world shine bright"

As Rishabh's words washed over them, Sarah and Juhi exchanged a knowing smile. Sarah gently explained, you see, in our family, there's no such thing as certain jobs being

assigned to specific people, like mummy can do this, pappa can do that." Rishab nodded in agreement, adding, "That's right. Just because mommy goes to work doesn't mean she can't cook or take care of the home, and just because daddy stays at home sometimes doesn't mean he can't work or take care of you."

Their daughter looked puzzled, so Sarah continued, "What we're trying to say is that everyone in our family can do any task they're capable of, regardless of whether they're a boy or a girl. Mommy and Daddy both have skills and interests that make them good at different things, and we support each other in sharing responsibilities."

Rishab chimed in, "For example, right now Daddy is at home with you because he enjoys spending time with you and wants to be involved in your life. But that doesn't mean he's not working. He can still do his work from home while being here for you." Sarah nodded, reinforcing the message. "Exactly. And just like Daddy can cook and clean, Mommy can work and fix things around the house. It's all about teamwork and supporting each other in whatever we do."

Their daughter's eyes lit up as she began to understand. "So, anyone can do anything if they try?" she asked.

"Exactly," Sarah replied with a smile. "And we want you to know that you can grow up to be anything you want to be, regardless of whether it's traditionally seen as a 'boy's' or 'girl's' job. The most important thing is to follow your passions and do what makes you happy."

As their daughter nodded in agreement, Sarah and Rishab shared a proud glance, grateful for the opportunity to instill such an important lesson in their young child.

In a world that was slowly but surely evolving, they had found their own path, guided by love, respect, and a shared vision of equality. And as they savoured the simple pleasures of family life, they knew that they were pioneers in a movement that was reshaping society for generations to come.

Chapter 11

# Embracing Solitude

---

Rhea had always been a social butterfly. She thrived in the company of others, feeding off the energy and connection she found in her friendships. But over time, Rhea began to feel a yearning for something more. She found herself craving solitude, a space to explore her own thoughts and desires without the distractions of others.

It was on a whim that Rhea decided to book a solo trip to Bali. The idea of traveling alone was both exhilarating and daunting, but she was determined to push herself out of her comfort zone.

Rhea stands in the bustling departure lounge of the airport, her large backpack slung over one shoulder and her carry-on in hand. She checks her phone one last time before turning it off, her excitement barely contained. The airport is a hive of activity, with travellers hurrying to their gates and announcements echoing over the PA system. Rhea finds a quiet corner and takes a deep breath, trying to calm the flutter of nerves in her stomach. She looks around at the sea of unfamiliar faces and feels a thrill of independence. As she heads towards the boarding gate, she pulls out her phone for a quick call to her parents.

Rhea: [Excitedly] "Hi Mom, hi Dad! Just wanted to let you know I'm about to board my flight to Bali!"

Mom: [Concerned] "Oh, Rhea! Are you sure you're okay traveling alone? Do you have everything you need?"

Rhea: [Reassuringly] "Yes, Mom, I'm all set. I've got my passport, tickets, and a list of emergency contacts. I'm a bit nervous, but it's going to be an adventure!"

Dad: [Encouragingly] "That's the spirit! Just make sure to keep in touch and let us know how it's going. Remember to stay safe and take lots of pictures."

Rhea: [Laughing] "I will! I promise. I'll call or text whenever I can. Don't worry too much; I'm sure it's going to be amazing."

Dad: [Fondly] "Love you, my child. Have a great trip, Rhea."

Rhea: [Hanging up] "Bye!"

Rhea hangs up with a smile, feeling a renewed sense of confidence as she heads towards the gate, ready to embark on her solo adventure.

As she boarded the plane, she felt a mix of excitement and trepidation, wondering what the next few days would bring.

As Rhea explored the bustling streets of Bali, she found herself slipping into a rhythm of exploration and self-discovery. She wandered through colourful markets, hiked through lush jungles, and lazed on tranquil beaches, all with a newfound sense of freedom and independence. With each passing day, Rhea felt herself shedding the insecurities and dependencies that had once held her back.

At night, Rhea would retreat to her cozy bungalow, where she would journal about her experiences and reflect on the lessons she had learned. She found solace in the quiet moments, relishing the opportunity to simply be with herself and her thoughts. And as she lay in bed, listening to the sounds of the jungle outside her window, she felt a deep sense of contentment wash over her.

Through her solo travels, Rhea discovered a new kind of strength within herself. She realized that she didn't need the constant validation and approval of others to feel whole. Instead, she found that true freedom came from within, from embracing her own company and learning to love herself unconditionally.

As Rhea boarded the plane back home, she felt a renewed sense of purpose and confidence. She knew that she would always cherish her friendships and connections with others, but she also knew that she had the power to stand on her own two feet, to chart her own path in the world. And she was excited to see where that path would lead her next. She found that she was enjoying the freedom and independence that came with being alone. She had the flexibility to go wherever she wanted, do whatever she pleased, and take the time to truly immerse herself in the places she visited.

While on board she was reading **Wild: From Lost to Found on the Pacific Crest Trail" by Cheryl Strayed** that reflects her journey and inner realization

*"I was lost, but I was on my way. I was walking through a landscape I'd never seen before. The wild, strange landscape of my own soul, and I was beginning to see the truth of who I really was. There was no map for this journey. No compass, no guidebook, no fellow travellers. I had to trust that my heart knew the way."*

She began to appreciate the solitude and the moments of introspection that came with being alone. She found herself

connecting more deeply with the people she met along the way, and forming meaningful relationships that she might not have had the opportunity to if she had been traveling with others.

Rhea realized that she didn't necessarily need to be surrounded by family or friends to enjoy her travels. And while she still missed the company of loved ones at times, she found that she was able to create her own sense of fulfilment and happiness on her solo adventures.

She began to see the world in a different light, and she embraced the changes that came with her newfound appreciation for solitude. She realized that being a social animal didn't necessarily mean always being surrounded by others, but rather finding connection and enjoyment in whatever form it may come.

So, as she continued her journey as a solo traveller, Rhea welcomed the changes and embraced the joy that came with experiencing the world on her own terms. And she found that she was truly content in her newfound sense of adventure and self-discovery.

# Chapter 12

# Pages of Change

---

Bill sat comfortably in his favourite armchair, the very one that had supported him through countless reading sessions. The room was a haven of literary history, with shelves stacked high with weathered books whose spines told stories of their own. The faint aroma of aged paper and ink hung in the air, a comforting reminder of afternoons spent in the company of literary greats. Across from him, his grandson Allan sprawled on the couch, absorbed in the glow of his tablet.

"Back in my day," Bill began, his voice tinged with nostalgia, "if you wanted to read a book, you had to go to the library."

Allan glanced up momentarily, his attention split between his grandfather and the digital world unfolding on his screen. "But now, we have eBooks," he countered. "You can carry hundreds of books with you wherever you go."

Bill waved his hand dismissively, a smile playing on his lips. "eBooks may be convenient, but there's something special about holding a physical book in your hands. Feeling the weight of it, turning the pages..."

Allan nodded, acknowledging the sentiment but eager to highlight the advantages of modern technology. "I get that, Grandpa. But with eBooks, you can adjust the font size, look up words instantly, and even read in the dark without a lamp."

Bill chuckled softly, his eyes reflecting a mix of amusement and nostalgia. "I suppose there are some advantages to these newfangled gadgets. But there's more to reading than just convenience. It's about the experience—the smell of the pages, the texture of the paper..."

"True," Allan conceded. "But times are changing, Grandpa. We have to adapt."

Bill gazed thoughtfully at the rows of books lining the walls. "Perhaps you're right, Allan. But there's one thing that will never change for me—the joy of wandering through the aisles of a library, surrounded by thousands of stories just waiting to be discovered." Rising from his armchair, he gestured for Allan to follow. "Come with me, Allan. I want to show you something."

Curiosity piqued, Allan set aside his tablet and followed his grandfather through the house to a room at the back. As they entered, Allan's eyes widened in awe. The room was a bibliophile's dream, with floor-to-ceiling bookshelves brimming with volumes of every imaginable genre.

"This," Bill declared with pride, "is my library."

Allan took in the sight, marvelling at the vast collection of literary treasures. Classic novels by Dickens and Austen stood beside thrilling mysteries by Agatha Christie, while timeless plays by Shakespeare adorned the shelves.

"Wow, Grandpa," Allan breathed, gently tracing his fingers along the spines of the books. "You have so many!"

Bill's eyes twinkled with pride as he surveyed his collection. "I've been collecting these books for decades. Each one holds a special place in my heart."

Allan's admiration deepened as he listened to his grandfather's words. "It's amazing to see how much you love reading, Grandpa."

Bill nodded, a wistful expression crossing his face. "These books have been my companions through good times and bad. They've transported me to far-off lands, introduced me to unforgettable characters, and taught me valuable lessons about life and love."

Allan was captivated, his curiosity intrigued. "But what about eBooks, Grandpa? Do you think they'll ever replace real books?"

Bill sighed, his gaze lingering on the cherished volumes. "Perhaps they will, someday. But for me, nothing can ever replace the feel of these books. These books are more than just stories—they're a part of who I am."

Allan's eyes softened with understanding. "I get it, Grandpa. And I think it's amazing that you've preserved these books for so long. They're like a treasure trove of wisdom and imagination."

Bill smiled, his heart swelling with pride. "Thank you, Allan. I'm glad you appreciate them. And who knows? Maybe one day, you'll pass them down to your own grandchildren."

With a shared sense of connection, grandfather and grandson stood side by side, enveloped in the timeless magic of books. Allan realized that while the world was changing, some things—like the deep bond formed through stories and the cherished memories they create—would remain constant.

As they settled into a comfortable silence, each lost in their own world of words—whether printed on paper or displayed on a screen—they understood that there was room for both. And in that quiet moment, Allan knew that the love for books, in whatever form they took, was a legacy worth cherishing and preserving for generations to come.

# Chapter 13

# Unbreakable Bonds

Kili and Jean gazed out the airplane window, their excitement palpable as the familiar skyline of their hometown came into view. It had been nearly a year since they last visited their parents and the anticipation of reuniting with family filled their hearts with warmth.

As the plane touched down and they made their way through the bustling airport, memories of childhood summers and holiday gatherings flooded their minds. For Kili, who had moved overseas with Jean and their two young children in pursuit of better career opportunities, these visits held a special significance—a chance to reconnect with their roots and the loved ones they left behind.

Kili's heart raced as he approached the familiar door of his childhood home. His mind swirled with a mix of anticipation and apprehension. Would his parents greet him with open arms, their love undiminished by the miles that separated them? Or would they struggle to conceal their disappointment, their emotions mirroring his own conflicted feelings about their distance?

But as soon as the door swung open and his parents enveloped him in a tight embrace, all of Kili's worries melted away. "Welcome home, son," his father said, his voice choked with emotion.

Inside, the familiar sights and sounds of home greeted them—a pot of stew simmering on the stove, the laughter of children playing in the backyard, and the comforting embrace of family.

Over dinner, Kili and Jean caught up with their parents, sharing stories of their life overseas and the adventures of their children. But despite the laughter and chatter, Kili couldn't shake the feeling of sadness that lingered in the air—a palpable sense of emptiness that seemed to weigh heavily on his parents' hearts. As the evening wore on, Kili's mother finally broached the subject that had been weighing on her mind. "We miss you, Kili," she said, her voice trembling with emotion. "We miss having you and your family close by, seeing your children grow up, being a part of their lives..."

Kili's heart ached at the rawness of his mother's words. He knew that their decision to move overseas had been difficult for their parents to accept, but he had never realized just how deeply it had affected them.

"We miss you too, Mom," Kili said, reaching out to grasp her hand. "And we're sorry for being so far away. But please know that you're always in our thoughts, and that we treasure every moment we get to spend together."

Jean nodded in agreement, her eyes shining with unshed tears. "Family is the most important thing in the world to us," she said softly. "And no matter where life takes us, we'll always find our way back home."

As the evening sun dipped below the horizon, casting a warm glow over the gathering of family members, Kili's parents and Jean's parents settled into their seats, cups of steaming tea in hand. The aroma of freshly baked cookies filled the air, mingling with the laughter and chatter of loved ones reunited.

With fond smiles, Kili's mother began to reminisce about the days when Kili was a young boy, growing up in the warmth of their joint family home. "I remember when Kili was just a little boy," she said, her eyes twinkling with nostalgia. "He was the centre of our world—the apple of our eye. We all doted on him and showered him with love and affection."

Kili's father his face creased with a smile. "Those were wonderful times," Kili's father smiled, his face adorned with gentle lines of joy and agreement., his voice tinged with wistfulness. "Living in a joint family, surrounded by the love and support of our extended family members—it was like a dream come true."

Jean's mother, her eyes sparkling with pride, chimed in, eager to share her own memories. "And Jean was no less," she said, her voice filled with admiration. "Even as a young girl, she was so responsible and caring. She would always lend a helping hand around the house, taking care of her younger siblings and cousins with such love and dedication."

As they sat together, sharing stories and laughter, Kili and Jean exchanged a knowing glance. They may have come from different backgrounds, but they shared a common bond—a deep-rooted love and appreciation for family. And as they listened to their parents reminisce about the joys of living in a joint family, they couldn't help but feel grateful for the love and support that had shaped their lives.

Kili and Jean's children listened intently to the stories of their parents' upbringing and the close bonds they shared with their grandparents; a curious expression spread across their faces. Finally, unable to contain their curiosity any longer, they turned to their parents with wide eyes.

"Mama, Papa," the eldest child, Emily, began tentatively, "why can't we stay with our grandparents like you did when you were little?"

Kili and Jean, understanding the earnestness behind their children's question. They had anticipated this conversation might come up eventually, but they hadn't quite prepared themselves for it.

"Well," Jean began, her voice gentle as she tried to find the right words, "it's not that we don't want to stay with our parents. It's just that things are a little different now." Kili added, reaching out to take Emily's hand. "You see, sweetheart, Grandma and Grandpa live far away from us. It's not easy for us to visit them as often as we'd like. "The younger child, Ethan, furrowed his brow in confusion. "But why can't they come and live with us then? Wouldn't that be nice?"

Kili and Jean exchanged another glance, touched by their children's innocence and longing for closer connections with their grandparents.

"We would love nothing more than to have Grandma and Grandpa live with us," Jean said softly, her voice tinged with emotion. "But sometimes, grown-ups have jobs and responsibilities that keep them busy. And sometimes, it's not possible for everyone to live together."

"But that doesn't mean we love Grandma and Grandpa any less," Kili added quickly, wanting to reassure his children. "We cherish every moment we get to spend with them, whether it's during our visits or through phone calls and video chats."

Emily and Ethan nodded, their young minds trying to make sense of the complexities of adulthood. Though they couldn't fully grasp the reasons behind their parents' explanations, they understood one thing—the love they shared with their grandparents knew no bounds, transcending time and distance. With hugs and reassurances, Kili and Jean comforted their children, promising to cherish the moments they shared as a family and to make the most of the precious time they had together, no matter the miles that separated them from their beloved grandparents.

As the stories of their parents' childhood unfolded before them, Emily and Ethan felt a mixture of joy and longing. They laughed at the mischievous antics their parents recounted

and marvelled at the deep connections they had with their grandparents. But alongside their happiness was a growing sense of curiosity and yearning.

"Why can't we have stories like these, Mama?" Emily asked, her eyes bright with excitement. "Why don't we get to spend as much time with Grandma and Grandpa?"

Jean's heart swelled with love for her children as she saw the longing in their eyes. She knelt beside them, wrapping them in a warm embrace. "Oh, my darlings," she murmured, her voice soft with emotion, "I wish we could have those stories too. But sometimes life takes us on different paths, and we have to make the best of the time we have."

Ethan frowned, his brows furrowing in confusion. "But why can't we see Grandma and Grandpa more often? Why do we have to be so far away from them?"

Kili knelt beside Jean, his heart heavy with the weight of his children's longing. "It's not that we don't want to see Grandma and Grandpa more often," he explained gently. "But sometimes things like work and school make it difficult for us to visit as often as we'd like."

Emily nodded slowly, trying to understand. "So, it's not because they don't love us?"

Kili and Jean exchanged a look, touched by their children's innocence and concern. "Oh, sweetie, no," Jean said, her voice filled with warmth. "Grandma and Grandpa love you very much. They think about you every day and wish they could be with you more often."

Ethan's eyes brightened at this revelation. "They do?"

"Yes, of course they do," Kili assured him with a smile. "And even though we can't be with them all the time, we can still keep them close in our hearts. We can share stories about them and the memories we've made together. And who knows? Maybe one day we'll all be together again."

Emily and Ethan smiled at each other, comforted by their parents' words. Though they still longed for more time with their grandparents, they took solace in the love that bound them together, across miles and years. And as they nestled into their parents' embrace, they knew that no matter where life took them, their family would always be their home.

The contrast between the generations becomes increasingly poignant as more families experience the same separation. For Kili's parents and many others of their generation, the ache of distance is tangible. Each passing day without the laughter of grandchildren echoing through the halls, without the warmth of family gatherings, only serves to deepen the sense of emptiness within their hearts.

Meanwhile, as younger generations, like Kili and Jean's, chase opportunities in distant lands, the connection to their roots gradually begins to fade. Initially driven by the promise of better prospects, they find themselves caught in the whirlwind of new experiences, forging a path separate from the traditions and closeness they once knew.

With each passing year, the divide widens. For the older generation, the yearning for the presence of loved ones becomes an ever-present ache, their homes echoing with the ghostly whispers of memories past. Meanwhile, for the younger generation, the bonds of family begin to fray, replaced by the demands of modern life and the pursuit of individual dreams.

Yet, amidst the growing chasm, there remains a thread of longing—a longing for the simplicity of days gone by, for the comfort of familiar faces and shared stories. And with passing days, both young and old alike find themselves grappling with the bittersweet reality of change—the pain of separation tempered by the enduring hope of reunion, and the knowledge that no matter the distance, the ties of family will always bind them together.

# Chapter 14

# Beyond Labels

In a peaceful neighbourhood, removed from the city's clamour, resided Preet and Jay—a couple whose love transcended conventional limits. Their bond was built not on societal expectations, but on a profound trust, understanding, and affection. Their paths had first crossed on a sunny afternoon in the city, leading them on a shared journey of exploration and personal growth.

Preet and Jay's relationship was unconventional by design. They found themselves questioning societal expectations and the traditional trajectory of commitment. For them, love was a living, breathing entity that couldn't be confined by conventional labels or institutions like marriage. Instead, they chose to embrace their relationship in its purest form, living together in a way that felt true and authentic to their hearts.

One evening, as the soft glow of twilight bathed the sky in hues of orange and pink, the residents of their condominium gathered for a community event. The atmosphere was warm and inviting, with neighbours exchanging pleasantries and sharing stories. Among them were Arun and Sunita, an older couple who had recently moved in, and Preet and Jay, who were eager to integrate into their new community.

As the evening progressed and conversations flowed, Arun found himself drawn to Preet and Jay. There was something in their demeanour—a quiet strength and understanding—that resonated with him. Over a casual chat, Arun began to share his own story, his voice tinged with nostalgia and emotion.

"It all began twenty-five years ago," Arun said, his eyes reflecting a depth of feeling. "Sunita and I were young and in love, so full of passion that we eloped, leaving behind everything familiar. We took a leap of faith, trusting in our love to guide us through the unknown."

As Arun spoke, the room seemed to pause, the gravity of his words creating a shared space of reflection. His gaze softened as he recalled their journey. "It wasn't always easy. We faced numerous challenges—societal expectations, financial struggles—but our love was a steadfast beacon. It guided us through the darkest times and illuminated our path forward."

Preet and Jay listened intently, moved by Arun's story. They could feel the resilience and depth of his love for Sunita, evident in every word he spoke.

"Now," Arun continued, his smile reflecting both pride and contentment, "we have two wonderful children and a lifetime of memories. Our journey hasn't been perfect, but every moment has been worth it."

As Arun's words settled, Preet and Jay looked at each other with a shared understanding. They had found more than just new neighbours in Arun and Sunita; they had found kindred spirits. Their bond was a reminder that love, in all its forms, was a powerful force that transcended conventional definitions.

Arun and Sunita's story was one of overcoming societal boundaries. Arun, from a modest background, and Sunita,

from a privileged family, had defied expectations to create a life together based on their love and determination.

As they shared a quiet moment, Jay turned to Arun and Sunita, his voice filled with reverence. "For Preet and me, our relationship has always been about more than societal norms. We've sought to define our own path, finding happiness in our unique connection rather than adhering to traditional expectations."

He looked at Preet, their hands intertwined—a symbol of their bond. "In each other's company, we've discovered a happiness that goes beyond conventions. We've embraced our relationship on our own terms, and that has brought us a sense of freedom and fulfilment."

Jay's words resonated with Arun and Sunita, who understood the essence of living authentically. The differences between their approaches to commitment highlighted the evolving perspectives on love and relationships.

As Arun and Sunita's 25th anniversary approached, they began planning a grand celebration—a reflection of their enduring commitment and their desire to share their joy with loved ones. Despite their distinct journeys, both couples celebrated their love, whether through traditional milestones or by forging their own paths.

In their hearts, Preet and Jay recognized that love was not confined by societal expectations but was a personal journey, uniquely defined by each couple. The shared understanding between Arun and Sunita reaffirmed that, no matter how paths diverged, the essence of love remained constant.

Their stories revealed a broader shift in societal attitudes—one where personal fulfilment and freedom were valued alongside traditional commitments. As they looked towards the future, both couples knew that their love would continue to guide them, providing strength and hope in a world ever-changing.

Chapter 15

# Boundless Horizons

Rashi found herself lost in the maze of Singapore's bustling streets, the city's neon lights casting a mesmerizing glow over her weary figure. It had been two years since she left her hometown in India, a decision she made from sheer necessity to support her struggling family back home. The promises of a better life in the city-state had lured her away, but reality had been far harsher than she could have imagined.

As she trudged home after a long day's work as a housemaid, her thoughts turned to Pawan, the man she had met not long after arriving in Singapore. At first, his attention had been a welcome distraction from the loneliness and hardship of her new life. As the weeks passed after their marriage, Rashi began to feel a growing sense of unease settling in the pit of her stomach. What had once seemed like the promise of a new beginning now felt like a heavy weight pressing down on her shoulders. Pawan's affection, once a source of comfort and reassurance, now felt suffocating, his love more possessive than genuine

Their days together were filled with awkward silences and forced smiles, the space between them growing wider with each passing moment. Rashi found herself longing for the freedom she had once taken for granted, the simple joys of her life before marriage now nothing more than distant memories.

And as she lay awake at night, her mind swirling with doubts and fears, Rashi couldn't shake the sinking feeling that she and Pawan were not meant to be together. Their differences, once overlooked in the heady rush of romance, now loomed large and insurmountable, casting a shadow over their fragile relationship.

One fateful evening, as she sat alone in her room, Rashi stumbled upon Raj in an online forum. Their connection was instant, their conversations a lifeline during her turmoil. Raj lived continents away, but distance seemed inconsequential in the face of their growing bond. They shared dreams, fears, and desires, their virtual connection deepening with each passing day.

On the other hand, she continued to go through the motions of married life, her smile becoming more strained with each passing day. But deep down, she knew that she could not continue to live a lie, that she owed it to herself to find the courage to pursue her own happiness, no matter the cost.

Rashi found herself drawn to Raj in a way she had never experienced with Pawan. His words were a balm to her weary soul, his gestures of affection a stark contrast to the suffocating love she had known before. As their relationship blossomed, she found herself drifting further and further away from her husband.

As the days passed, Rashi and Raj's bond grew stronger, their conversations a lifeline amid their respective struggles.

By now Rashi knew that she had to find the strength to break free from the chains that bound her to a loveless marriage. For only then could she hope to find the happiness and fulfilment she so desperately craved.

One evening, as they sat in front of their respective screens, miles apart yet closer than ever in heart, Raj broke the silence, "Rashi, do you ever feel like we're living in a dream? Sometimes, I can't believe how lucky I am to have found you." Rashi's heart swelled at his words, a smile tugging at the corners of her lips, "I know what you mean, Raj. Sometimes, it feels like fate brought us together, like we were always meant to find each other."

Their eyes locked through the glow of their screens, a shared understanding passing between them.

"I long for the moment when we no longer have to part ways, When I can hold you in my arms and never let you go. "Raj expressed ardently.

Rashi's breath caught in her throat at the thought of being with Raj in person, the distance between them suddenly felt unbearable.

"I share that sentiment, Raj. But for now, let's cherish every moment we have, even if it's only through the glow of our screens," Rashi responded, infused with emotion.

Their conversation continued late into the night, their laughter and whispered promises a through to the strength of their love.

As they said their goodbyes and logged off for the night, Rashi couldn't help but feel a sense of longing deep within her heart. But she knew that no matter the distance between them, their love would always find a way to bridge the gap.

But with Raj came guilt, a nagging voice in the back of her mind reminding her of the promises she had made to Pawan. As the days turned into weeks and the weeks into months, her love for Raj only grew stronger, eclipsing any doubts or reservations she may have had.

When Raj announced his plans to visit Singapore, Rashi's heart skipped a beat. It was a risk she knew she shouldn't take, but the lure of his presence was too powerful to resist. Their reunion was everything she had hoped for and more, their stolen moments together a fleeting taste of the happiness she craved.

But as their affair continued, Rashi found herself consumed by guilt and uncertainty. She knew that what she was doing was wrong, that she was betraying the trust of the man who had once promised her his love. Yet, in Raj's arms,

all thoughts of right and wrong melted away, replaced by a love so intoxicating it left her breathless.

Eventually, Rashi made the decision to confront the reality that she harboured no feelings or love for Pawan. She spoke of her desire to start anew, to leave behind the wreckage of their failed marriage and seek happiness elsewhere.

And so, with Pawan's reluctant blessing, Rashi boarded a plane bound for the United States, her heart heavy with guilt yet hopeful for the future that awaited her with Raj.

The anticipation hung thick in the air as Rashi stood nervously at the arrivals gate of the airport, her heart pounding in her chest. She scanned the crowd anxiously, searching for the face she had only seen through a screen, the man who had captured her heart from thousands of miles away.

And then, amidst the throng of travellers, she saw him – Raj, his eyes searching the crowd with a mixture of excitement and nervousness mirroring her own. Their eyes met, and in that moment, everything else faded away, leaving only the two of them standing in a world of their own.

Raj approached her slowly, his steps hesitant yet determined, until finally, he stood before her, a smile spreading across his face.

Rashi felt her breath catch in her throat as she looked up at him, her heart swelling with emotion.

They stood there for a moment, simply drinking in each other's presence, the impact of their shared journey lingered between them, palpable and real.

And then, without a word, Raj reached out and took her hand in his, his touch sending a jolt of electricity coursing through her veins. Their eyes locked in a silent exchange of understanding, their unspoken feelings echoing in the space between them.

Rashi nodded eagerly, her heart soaring with excitement at the prospect of exploring this new chapter of their lives together.

And with that, hand in hand, they walked out of the airport and into the world, their love shining bright like a beacon in the darkness, guiding them towards their shared future.

After a few days, they exchanged vows in a small temple overlooking the city skyline, Rashi felt a sense of peace wash over her, the weight of her past finally lifted from her shoulders. With Raj by her side, she knew that she had found the love she had been searching for, a love that transcended boundaries and defied all odds.

As Rashi settled into her new life in the United States, the reality of her transformation from a small-town housemaid to the cherished queen of Raj's heart felt like a dream she never dared to imagine. The bustling streets of Singapore were now a distant memory, replaced by the sprawling landscapes and vibrant cities of her new home. As she gazed out of the window of their cozy apartment, Rashi couldn't help but marvel at the twists and turns fate had thrown her way. Never in her wildest dreams did she imagine that she would become a citizen of the United States, let alone find true love in the arms of a man who cherished her like no other.

Amidst the whirlwind of their newfound happiness, Rashi couldn't shake the lingering sense of disbelief that still lingered in the depths of her heart. How had she, a simple girl from a small town in India, found herself living a life she had only ever read about in fairy tales? But as she looked into Raj's eyes, she knew that it didn't matter how they had gotten here, what mattered was the love they shared, a love that had defied all odds and transcended every obstacle in their path.

Despite the doubts and uncertainties that had once plagued her mind, she had come to realize that not all distant relationships were doomed to failure, nor were all relationships formed through the internet fraudulent or insincere. And as she looked around at the life they had built together – their cozy apartment, the laughter that filled their home, and the shared moments of tenderness and affection – Rashi knew that their love was as real and genuine as any she had ever known.

But more than that, she had come to realize that the internet, despite its pitfalls and dangers, could also be a source of genuine connection and companionship. Through the screen of her laptop, she had found a kindred spirit in Raj, someone who saw her for who she truly was and accepted her without reservation. Their love had blossomed in the digital realm, nurtured by countless messages, video calls, and virtual embraces. And while she knew that their journey had been unconventional, she also knew that it had been undeniably real.

As she wrapped her arms around Raj and felt the warmth of his embrace, she knew that their love would only continue to grow stronger, a beacon of hope and possibility in a world often fraught with doubt and uncertainty.

Chapter 16

## A Fragile Balance

---

In the quiet suburbs of a bustling city, Mark and Sarah lived with their son, Ethan, who was diagnosed with autism at a young age. As Ethan grew, so did the challenges that came with his care, putting immense pressure on Mark and Sarah's personal and professional lives.

Mark, a dedicated architect, found himself torn between the demands of his career and the needs of his son. Deadlines loomed overhead like dark clouds, threatening to unleash a storm of missed opportunities and lost clients. Every evening, Mark would leave the office with a heavy heart, knowing that he was leaving behind unfinished work to tend to Ethan's needs. The guilt gnawed at him, a relentless reminder of the delicate balance he struggled to maintain between his passion for architecture and his commitment to his family.

Sarah, a talented writer, faced a different set of challenges in her professional life. Freelancing offered her the flexibility to be there for Ethan when he needed her most, but it also meant running around a maze of uncertainty and instability. Deadlines blurred together in a whirlwind of stress and anxiety, each one accompanied by the ever-present fear of falling short and losing out on future opportunities. Amidst the chaos, Sarah found solace in the words she penned, each sentence a reflection of her resilience and strength she drew from her experiences as a mother of a special child.

Their personal lives bore the brunt of the pressure as well. Date nights became a rare luxury, overshadowed by the constant worry and exhaustion that accompanied raising a special needs child. Friends drifted away, unable to understand the challenges they faced or the sacrifices they made daily. Mark and Sarah found strength in each other, their love serving as a beacon of hope in the darkest of times.

But perhaps the greatest challenge they faced was the uncertainty of the future. What would happen to Ethan as he grew older? Would he be able to find a world that often seemed too harsh and unforgiving? These questions weighed heavily on Mark and Sarah's hearts, their minds haunted by visions of a future filled with unknowns and unanswered prayers.

It was a bright, crisp morning, the kind that promised the start of a beautiful day. Sarah woke up feeling a sense of contentment, the warm embrace of her husband Mark comforting her as she stretched beneath the covers. But as she stirred awake, she noticed a heaviness in the air, a tension that seemed to linger like a shadow over their bed.

Mark sat beside her, his expression grave as he gently took her hand in his. Sarah's heart skipped a beat at the seriousness in his eyes, a knot of apprehension forming in the pit of her stomach.

"Sarah," Mark began, his voice trembling with emotion, "there's something I need to tell you."

Her heart pounding in her chest, Sarah listened as Mark delivered the devastating news—the diagnosis that would change their lives forever. Terminal illness. The words hung in the air like a heavy fog, obscuring the bright promise of the day with a shroud of uncertainty and fear.

As the reality of her diagnosis sank in, Sarah felt a wave of emotions crashing over her like a tidal wave. Fear, anger, sorrow—all swirling together in a tempest of confusion and despair.

Together, they faced the daunting journey that lay ahead, maneuvering through the labyrinth path of treatments and appointments with a quiet determination born of love and resilience.

Sarah lay in her bed, her breathing laboured and shallow, the lines of pain etched upon her face. Mark sat beside her, his hand clasping hers tightly, as if afraid to let go. Their eyes met, a silent exchange of love and understanding passing between them, as they braced themselves for the inevitable.

The room was hushed, the only sound the soft murmur of distant voices and the rhythmic beeping of machines. Outside, the world continued, oblivious to the quiet tragedy unfolding within the walls of their home.

As the hours passed, Sarah's breathing grew fainter, her grip on life slipping away like grains of sand through an hourglass. Mark watched helplessly, his heart breaking with each shallow breath she took, his own tears mingling with hers as they fell in silent sorrow.

And then, in the blink of an eye, she was gone. The room seemed to grow still, as if holding its breath in reverence for the life that had passed. Mark's sobs echoed in the silence, a symphony of grief that reverberated through the empty space.

As Mark sat beside his beloved wife for the last time, he whispered words of love and farewell, his heart heavy with the weight of grief yet buoyed by the knowledge that she was finally at peace.

The loss of Sarah left Mark shattered, his world crumbling around him like a fragile house of cards. As he struggled to come to terms with her terminal illness, a suffocating sense of burden settled over him like a heavy cloak, threatening to drown him in its burden.

Mark's love for Ethan remained uncompromised, a beacon of light in the darkness that consumed him. But with Sarah gone, the responsibilities of caring for their son became overwhelming, a relentless tide that threatened to pull him under. He felt as though all the doors to hope had

closed, leaving him trapped in a suffocating cycle of grief and despair.

In a moment of desperation, Mark made the agonizing decision to send Ethan to a hostel for special needs children. The feeling of guilt devoured him, but he consoled that this sacrifice he had made in the name of his own sanity. He told himself it was for the best, that Ethan would receive the care and support he needed in a structured environment.

In the days that followed, Mark found himself adrift in a sea of emptiness, his home echoing with the absence of his beloved wife and son. But slowly, as the days turned into weeks and the weeks into months, he began to rediscover himself amidst the ruins of his shattered life.

He threw himself into his work with a renewed sense of purpose, finding space in the beauty of architecture and the promise of a future filled with endless possibilities. And though the pain of losing Sarah and sending Ethan away never truly faded, he found comfort in the knowledge that they were both in a better place, free from the burdens that had weighed them down in life. As as he looked out at the world with fresh eyes, Mark realized that the doors to hope had never truly closed. They had simply been waiting for him to find the courage to open them once again, to embrace the future with open arms and a heart filled with love.

For in the end, it was not the tragedies we faced that defined us, but the strength and resilience with which we rose from the ashes, ready to face whatever challenges lay ahead. And as Mark stepped into the light of a new day, he knew that Sarah and Ethan would always be with him, guiding him along the path to healing and redemption.

# Chapter 17

# Changing Tides of Tradition

Finally, Jyostna arrived at her ancestral home, where her extended family eagerly awaited her return. Stepping through the threshold, she was enveloped in warmth and love, greeted by hugs and laughter from her cousins, aunts, and uncles. It had been four long years since she left Kolkata to pursue her medical studies in Ireland. Now, as she returned home during Durga Puja, the festival she had missed dearly, she couldn't contain her anticipation.

While on her way home Joystna felt a peculiar mix of nostalgia and novelty. The familiar sights, sounds, and smells enveloped her, evoking memories of the home she had departed from. However, amidst the comforting familiarity, she couldn't help but notice subtle changes. The roads, once spacious and open, now seemed more congested, crowded with vehicles and pedestrians alike. New residential areas had sprung up, altering the city's skyline and adding a layer of unfamiliarity to the landscape. Despite these changes, Kolkata retained its essence, still pulsating with life and energy, welcoming Joystna back with open arms in the festive mood of Durga Pooja.

Growing up in a joint family, she had always been surrounded by the hustle and bustle of relatives coming and going, the constant chatter and laughter echoing through the halls. But now, there was a noticeable shift – a quietness that hung in the air, a distance that seemed to have crept in. Her cousins, once her closest confidants, seemed different somehow. They no longer shared the same bond they once did, their interests and priorities diverging over the years. It pained her to realize that they had grown apart during her absence, their connection weakened by the passage of time.

As Jyostna unpacked her belongings and distributed souvenirs she had brought from Ireland for each family member, Jyostna's mother was busy in the kitchen. The savoury aroma of spices filled the air as she prepared Jyostna's favourite dishes, ones she had dearly missed during her years away. Each clatter of utensils and sizzle of ingredients seemed to echo the warmth and love that her mother poured into every dish, a tangible expression of welcome and affection for her beloved daughter's return. After all, Bengalis are known as "bhojon priyo bangali" as Bengalis celebrate the essence of Bengali culture through its deep-rooted love for food. Each dish tells a story, reflecting the region's history, agricultural abundance, and cultural heritage. However, the significance extends beyond mere food; it's a way of life, a source of pride, and a means of connection to their roots. It's about savouring every bite, cherishing every moment, and honouring the culinary legacy passed down through generations.

Jyotsna must have been overwhelmed with nostalgia as she savoured the traditional Bengali delicacies lovingly prepared by her mother. Each dish would have carried with it memories of past Durga Puja celebrations, family gatherings, and moments spent with loved ones. The aroma of '*basanti pulao*', the richness of '*kosha mangsho*', the delicate flavors of '*bhapa ilish*', and the comforting familiarity of '*jhuri aloo bhaja*' would have transported her back to her childhood home. The warmth of her mother's cooking would have made

her feel cherished and loved, reaffirming the importance of family and tradition in her life.

As Sasthi (sixth day of Durga pooja) approached, she observed the preparations for the festival, she couldn't help but notice a change in the air. The excitement that once filled the household seemed muted, replaced by a sense of routine and complacency. Gone were the days of eagerly selecting new outfits for Durga Pujo, of scouring the markets for the latest trends. Instead, her family members now preferred the convenience of online shopping, choosing practicality over tradition. Jyostna's mother was ready with a traditional red and white saree for 'Pushpanjali" – prayer to Goddess

Durga. She did get a beautiful 'tant' saree for Jyostna as well so that she can join the pujo with new traditional saree, she found reassurance in the familiar rituals of durga pujo – the scent of incense wafting through the air, the sound of 'dhak' drums reverberating in the distance, the sight of the majestic goddess Durga adorning pandals across the city.

Surrounded by the familiar faces of her family members and the comforting smells of home-cooked food, Jyotsna would have felt a deep sense of belonging and gratitude for the opportunity to reunite with her loved ones and partake in the joyous festivities of durga pujo once again.

As she sat with her elders, sipping on steaming cups of chai, she listened to their conversations with a heavy heart. Gone were the days of eagerly donning their finest attire and braving the crowded streets to witness the grandeur of the puja pandals. Instead, they now preferred the comfort of their own homes, watching live streams of the festivities from the safety of their living rooms. Jyostna couldn't help but notice the shifting dynamics within her family. Once, the entire clan would eagerly embark on pandal hopping adventures, revelling in the sights and sounds of the festival. But now, things are different.

With age comes wisdom, and with wisdom comes the desire for peace and tranquillity. The elderly members of her family had seen their fair share of pandal hopping adventures, and now, they longed for a quieter, more subdued celebration. But for Jyostna's cousins, the allure of social media was too strong to resist. As they eagerly donned their trendy outfits and set out to explore the pandals, their primary motivation seemed to be capturing the perfect social media photo rather than immersing themselves in the true essence of the festival.

It was a stark reminder of how technology had infiltrated every aspect of their lives, reshaping traditions and priorities in its wake. Once, Durga Pujo had been a time for family bonding and togetherness, a time to strengthen the bonds that held them together. But now, it seemed that the festival had become little more than a backdrop for social media updates and status symbols. As Jyostna reflected on the changing tides of tradition, she couldn't help but feel a sense of loss. The vibrant fabric of family connections that once defined Durga Pujo had begun to fray, replaced by a digital facsimile of togetherness.

Amidst the chaos and confusion, she clung to the hope that the true spirit of the festival would endure – that beneath the surface, beyond the glare of screens and the allure of social media, there still lay the heart and soul of Durga Pujo, waiting to be rediscovered by those who dared to seek it.

Sitting by her room window, Jyostna gazed out at the familiar street scene, her heart heavy with nostalgia. Where once stood Dulal Kaku's beloved *"paan & cha gumti,"* a quaint hut-shaped shop selling beetle leaf and tea, now lay an empty space, devoid of its former charm. She had grown up watching Dulal Kaku tirelessly serving customers, his warm smile and friendly banter a fixture of her childhood memories. But with Kaku's passing during the height of the Covid pandemic, his son had sought better opportunities in Dubai, leaving behind the legacy of the family business. Now, the once bustling spot had been claimed by a contractor, erasing all traces of the cherished gathering place that had been a cornerstone of the neighbourhood for so many years.

A whirlwind of emotions swirling within her as she reflected on the past four years spent away from home for her studies. While she had pursued her dream of excelling in medicine, a goal she had always harboured since childhood, she couldn't shake the feeling of loss for the time she had missed with her family and the changes that had occurred in her absence. Despite the academic achievements and personal growth she had gained during her time abroad, there was a part of her that longed for the familiarity and warmth of her homeland. The dream of practicing medicine in India had always been her ultimate aspiration, but now, as she grappled with the reality of her return, she couldn't help but feel a tinge of uncertainty mingled with the excitement of pursuing her passion on home soil.

Chapter 18

# Exploring Perspectives

The crackling flames of the campfire danced in the night as five teenagers sat around, their faces illuminated by its warm glow. They had embarked on a seven-day summer camp, eager for adventure and excitement. Little did they know, the most enlightening moments would come from the conversations they shared beneath the starry sky.

As they roasted marshmallows and swapped stories, the topic turned to the meaning of success. Each teen had a different perspective, shaped by their unique experiences and aspirations. For Akshay, success meant achieving academic excellence and securing a stable career, a notion instilled by his parents from a young age. Maya, on the other hand, believed success was about following her passions and making a positive impact on the world, even if it meant taking unconventional paths.

Their discussions soon delved deeper, touching upon the challenges they faced in communicating with their parents. Arjun expressed frustration at his parents' lack of understanding regarding his interests and ambitions, feeling pressured to conform to their expectations rather than pursue his own dreams. Riya nodded in agreement, sharing her own struggles in expressing her desires for the future without feeling judged or dismissed by her family.

As the night wore on, their conversations grew more introspective, pondering the uncertainties of adulthood and the paths they hoped to forge for themselves. They voiced their fears and insecurities, wondering if they would ever have the freedom to pursue their passions without fear of judgment or failure.

But amidst their doubts, a sense of solidarity emerged, binding them together in shared hopes and aspirations. They realized that while their journeys may be different, they were united by a common desire for understanding, acceptance, and the freedom to pursue their dreams.

Underneath the vast expanse of the starlit sky, four teenagers found strength in each other's company, knowing that no matter what challenges lay ahead, they would face them together, guided by the light of their shared dreams and aspirations.

Raj, the embodiment of a carefree spirit, exuded an aura of happiness wherever he went. While others fretted about the future, he lived in the present, embracing each moment with unbridled enthusiasm. Despite the occasional pressures from teachers and parents to excel academically, Raj remained steadfast in his belief that true fulfillment lay in pursuing happiness above all else.

As the campfire crackled and conversation flowed, Raj shared his perspective with his friends. He confessed to feeling like a mediocre student, never quite meeting the lofty expectations set by others. Yet, in the same breath, he expressed contentment with his lot in life. For Raj, success was not measured in grades or accolades, but in the simple joys of laughter, friendship, and a vibrant social life.

His words resonated with his friends, sparking a lively discussion about the true meaning of success. While some argued for academic achievement and financial stability, others, like Raj, championed the pursuit of happiness and fulfillment. In a world consumed by ambition and competition, Raj's carefree outlook served as a refreshing reminder to cherish the present moment and find joy in the journey, no matter where it may lead.

Riya's words hung in the air; her concern palpable as she voiced the anxieties that had been weighing on her mind. Raj listened attentively; his carefree demeanor momentarily softened by her earnest question. He pondered her words thoughtfully before responding.

"Riya, I understand where you're coming from, and your concerns are valid," Raj began, his voice tinged with sincerity. "But I truly believe that happiness isn't solely dependent on material wealth or professional success. Yes, there may come a time when I must support myself and my family, and I'm prepared to face that challenge when it arises. However, I also believe that true happiness comes from living authentically, pursuing my passions, and nurturing meaningful relationships."

He paused, searching Riya's eyes for understanding. "I may not have grand ambitions or aspirations for immense wealth, but that doesn't mean I'm resigned to a life of mediocrity. I have dreams and goals, just like everyone else. And while they may not align with society's conventional measures of success, they are no less valid or meaningful to me."

Riya nodded; her expression softened by Raj's words. In that moment, she understood that happiness was a deeply personal journey, one that could not be defined by external standards or expectations.

Akshay's dissenting voice added a layer of tension to the conversation, his concern for Raj's future palpable in his words. "Raj, I understand your perspective, but in today's competitive world, academic excellence often opens doors to opportunities that might otherwise remain closed. Without strong grades and prestigious credentials, you may find it challenging to compete the professional landscape and achieve your goals."

Raj nodded thoughtfully, acknowledging Akshay's valid point. "You're right, Akshay. The competition is fierce, and the pressure to excel can feel overwhelming at times. But for me, happiness and fulfillment are not synonymous with academic achievements or societal expectations. I believe in carving out my own path, one that aligns with my values and passions."

He paused, a flicker of uncertainty crossing his face. "Perhaps I'm being idealistic, and there may come a time when I'll need to reassess my approach. But for now, I'm content to follow my heart and trust in my ability to find my way, no matter the challenges that lie ahead."

Arjun's question about Raj's parents prompted a thoughtful response, tinged with a mixture of appreciation and resignation. "My parents, like many others, certainly have expectations for me based on their own experiences and values," Raj admitted. "They've worked hard to provide for our family and naturally want me to succeed in a similar fashion. However, they've never resorted to coercion or undue pressure. They encourage me to do my best but ultimately respect my autonomy and individuality."

He paused, a hint of wistfulness in his tone. "My family is fortunate, with successful careers and financial stability.

They envision a similar path for me, but I can't say with certainty whether I'll follow in their footsteps. What I do know is that I refuse to sacrifice the meaningful connections in my life – friendships, social experiences, and time with loved ones – for the sake of societal expectations or the pursuit of accolades."

With a shrug, Raj added, "I prioritize what brings me joy and fulfillment, whether it's investing time in my appearance, nurturing friendships, or simply enjoying the present moment. As for the future, well, I'll cross that bridge when I come to it." His words carried a sense of resolve, a quiet determination to live life on his own terms, unfettered by the constraints of conventional success.

Raj's question directed at Maya shifted the focus of the conversation to her aspirations and passions. Maya, with a contemplative expression, took a moment to collect her thoughts before responding.

"Well, Raj, I've always been drawn to the arts – music, painting, writing. There's something incredibly freeing about creative expression, something that resonates deep within me," Maya began, her eyes lighting up with enthusiasm. "For as long as I can remember, I've dreamt of pursuing a career in the arts, whether it's composing music, illustrating children's books, or writing poetry."

She paused, a smile playing at the corners of her lips. "I know it's not the most conventional path, and there are certainly challenges and uncertainties that come with it. But for me, the possibility of following my passion and making a meaningful impact through my art outweighs any doubts or fears."

As she spoke, Maya's passion for the arts radiated from her, infusing the conversation with a sense of possibility and inspiration. And though the road ahead may be uncertain, one thing was clear – Maya was determined to pursue her dreams with dedication and conviction.

Raj's follow-up question delved deeper into Maya's resolve and determination. Maya paused, considering his inquiry with a thoughtful expression.

"I'm fortunate to have supportive parents who have always encouraged me to pursue my passions, even if they stray from the conventional path," Maya replied, gratitude evident in her voice. "But if, for some reason, they were

to withdraw their support, it wouldn't diminish my determination to follow my dreams. At the end of the day, the decision to pursue my passion lies within me, and I'm willing to take on whatever challenges may come my way."

A quiet resolve settled over Maya as she spoke, her words echoing with unwavering determination. "I believe in the power of my dreams and my ability to make them a reality. And no matter the obstacles I may face, I'll continue to forge ahead with courage and conviction, fueled by my love for the arts."

Raj's anecdote painted a poignant picture of the struggles faced by his friend, highlighting the importance of parental understanding and support in nurturing a child's passions and well-being. As he recounted the story, a sombre mood settled over the group, each teenager reflecting on the implications of such experiences.

"It's heartbreaking to hear stories like that," Raj continued, his voice tinged with empathy. "But it also serves as a background of the profound impact parents can have on their children's lives. It's crucial for parents to recognize and validate their children's interests and aspirations, even if they diverge from the conventional path."

He recounted how, through a compassionate teacher's intervention and his own efforts to reach out, his friend found support in sharing his struggles. "Sometimes, all it takes is a listening ear and a willingness to understand," Raj remarked, his words carrying a weight of wisdom beyond his years.

As the campfire crackled and the night stretched on, Raj's story lingered in the air, a reflection of the importance of open communication and empathy in discussing the complexities of adolescence.

Arjun's frustration with parental rigidity struck a chord with the group, prompting Raj to offer his own insights on effective communication with parents. "You're right, Arjun. It can be tough when parents seem set in their ways," Raj acknowledged, nodding sympathetically. "But sometimes, just listening to their perspective can make a difference. Even if we don't agree with them, showing them that we're willing to hear them out can open the door to more productive conversations."

He continued, sharing his own experiences of going through challenging discussions with his parents. "I've been there, too. It's not always easy, but I've found that acknowledging their point of view, even if I don't agree with it, can help ease tensions and create space for dialogue."

Raj then suggested seeking support from school counsellors as a valuable resource for bridging communication gaps between teens and their parents. "Most schools have counsellors who are trained to help students to understand difficult situations," he explained. "If you're struggling to communicate with your parents, don't hesitate to reach out to them. They can provide guidance and support to help you express yourself and find common ground with your parents."

As his words resonated with his friends, Raj hoped they would take his advice to heart, knowing that effective communication was key to fostering understanding and harmony within families.

Raj's confession about his nighttime habits sparked a thoughtful discussion among the group, touching on the delicate balance between parental guidance and personal autonomy. As Raj explained his nightly routine and his parents' concerns about his sleep schedule, his friends nodded in understanding, recognizing similar struggles in their own lives.

"It's definitely a tricky situation," Maya remarked, her brow furrowed in contemplation. "On one hand, we want to assert our independence and make decisions for ourselves. But on the other hand, our parents have our best interests at heart, even if we don't always see eye to eye with them."

Arjun chimed in, sharing his own experiences of butting heads with his parents over rules and restrictions. "I get where you're coming from, Raj. Sometimes it feels like our parents are just trying to control us, but deep down, they only want what's best for us," he admitted, a hint of resignation in his voice.

Raj nodded in agreement, acknowledging the wisdom in his friends' words. "Exactly. It's easy to brush off our parents' advice as nagging or interference, but they've been through it all before and they have valuable insights to offer," he reflected. "At the end of the day, it's about finding a balance between asserting our independence and respecting their guidance."

In Kahlil Gibran's -The Prophet, he emphasizes the autonomy of children and their connection to the future, which belongs to them rather than their parents. The idea is that youth are independent beings with their own destinies, and they are the ones who will shape the future, often in ways that those from previous generations may not fully comprehend or control.

*"Your children are not your children.*

*They are the sons and daughters of Life's longing for itself.*

*They come through you but not from you,*

*And though they are with you yet they belong not to you.*

*You may give them your love but not your thoughts,*

*For they have their own thoughts.*

*You may house their bodies but not their souls,*

*For their souls dwell in the house of tomorrow,*

*which you cannot visit, not even in your dreams.*

*You may strive to be like them,*

*but seek not to make them like you.*

*For life goes not backward nor tarries with yesterday."*

# Chapter 19

# Caught in the Web

Eva, a bright young adult, stepped into the workforce with dreams of success and fulfilment after completing her studies at university. Armed with ambition and enthusiasm, she adorned the professional world with vigour, eager to make her mark.

Eva became increasingly enchanted by the attraction of social media. The thrill of receiving likes and comments on her posts became a source of validation and self-worth, gradually consuming more and more of her time and attention.

At first, it seemed harmless – a fleeting distraction from the stresses of work and life. But as Eva's obsession with social media grew, so too did its detrimental effects on her well-being. She found herself constantly comparing her life to the carefully curated images of perfection portrayed on her feed, leading to feelings of inadequacy and self-doubt.

Caught in the endless cycle of seeking validation through likes and comments, Eva's work began to suffer. She struggled to focus, constantly checking her phone for updates and losing precious hours to mindless scrolling. Deadlines were missed, projects fell behind, and her once-promising career began to unravel before her eyes. There came a moment when Eva posted something on social media that violated company policies, putting her job in jeopardy. Panicked and anxious about the consequences, Eva knew she had to act swiftly and decisively. Recognizing her mistake, she immediately deleted the post and issued a sincere apology, acknowledging her lapse in judgment and committing to upholding the company's values in the future. Taking proactive steps to mitigate the damage, Eva also reached out to her supervisor to explain the situation candidly and express her remorse. Though the repercussions were inevitable, Eva's willingness to take responsibility for her actions and demonstrate genuine contrition earned her a measure of respect and goodwill from her employer.

Outside of work, Eva's personal life also began to unravel. Relationships faltered as she prioritized her online persona over real-life connections, unable to escape the grip of social media's artificial allure. As Eva's life spiralled out of control, she was forced to confront the harsh reality of her addiction to social media. What had once seemed like harmless fun had morphed into a destructive force, wreaking havoc on every aspect of her existence.

Eva confided in her close friend, seeking guidance on how to break free from the digital web that ensnared her. Together, they brainstormed strategies to reclaim control over her life. Her friend suggested setting strict boundaries for social media usage, allocating specific times of the day for checking notifications and engaging online. Additionally, they explored alternative hobbies and activities that would divert Eva's attention away from the addictive allure of social media, such as exercising, reading, or pursuing creative outlets. With her friend's support and practical advice, Eva felt empowered to take the first steps toward liberation from the digital trap.

Slowly but surely, Eva began to reclaim control over her life, breaking free from the shackles of social media and

rediscovering the beauty of living in the present moment. She discovered a newfound sense of balance and perspective, she realized that true happiness could never be found in the fleeting validation of likes and comments, but in the richness of authentic human connection and the pursuit of genuine passion and purpose.

Eva, determined to reclaim control over her online presence, embarked on a new chapter of her social media journey. Instead of succumbing to the allure of superficial content and shallow validation, she chose to use her platform as a means of inspiration and empowerment. With courage and authenticity, Eva began sharing her success stories and personal triumphs, offering glimpses into her life after entering the workforce. Through heartfelt captions and candid reflections, she documented her journey of growth, resilience, and self-discovery, inspiring others to pursue their dreams and overcome obstacles with determination and grace.

As Eva continued to share her journey on social media, she remained true to herself, refusing to compromise her values or authenticity for the sake of popularity or approval. With each post, she reaffirmed her commitment to using her voice and platform for good, spreading positivity, encouragement, and hope in a world often clouded by negativity and self-doubt.

And as her online community grew, so too did Eva's sense of purpose and fulfilment. She had discovered that true success wasn't measured in likes or followers, but in the lives, she touched and the hearts she inspired along the way. Eva embraced her role as a beacon of light in the often-murky waters of social media, illuminating the path for others to find their own voices and shine brightly in their unique brilliance.

The pervasive addiction to social media among teens, young adults, and adults raises important questions about its long-term impact on future generations. While social media offers valuable opportunities for learning, connection, and self-expression, there is also a darker side characterized by shallow content, sensationalism, and exploitation. The rise of content creators who prioritize shock value and sensationalism over substance is indeed troubling. By resorting to tactics like body show-offs and other attention-grabbing strategies to garner popularity and financial gain, these creators contribute to a culture of superficiality and instant gratification. This trend not only normalizes unhealthy behaviours but also perpetuates unrealistic standards of beauty, success, and happiness, particularly among impressionable youth.

The consequences of this phenomenon are far-reaching and potentially damaging. Exposure to such content can distort young minds' perceptions of self-worth, fuelling insecurities and fostering unhealthy comparison with others. Moreover, the relentless pursuit of likes, followers, and validation on social media can erode real-life relationships, contribute to feelings of loneliness and isolation, and detract from meaningful pursuits and experiences.

As we contemplate the implications for future generations, it's essential to recognize the need for greater awareness and critical thinking skills. Educating young people about media literacy, digital citizenship, and healthy online behaviours is paramount to empowering them to understand the digital landscape responsibly and discerningly. Equipping them with the tools to question, evaluate, and resist the influence of harmful content is crucial in fostering a generation that values authenticity, empathy, and genuine connection.

The impact of social media on future generations will depend on how we choose to address these challenges. By promoting media literacy, fostering open dialogue, and advocating for ethical and responsible use of social media, we can strive to create a digital environment that uplifts and empowers rather than exploits and diminishes.

Here is a quote from "The Great Gatsby" by F. Scott Fitzgerald:

"*So, we beat on, boats against the current, borne back ceaselessly into the past*", mirrors the challenge of moving forward in life while being continuously drawn back by old habits, akin to Eva's struggle with her social media addiction.

# Alone Together

The sun dipped low on the horizon, casting long shadows over the quiet suburban street where Revanna and Rihaana lived. The air was heavy with the scent of spring blossoms, a stark contrast to the heaviness that had settled in the hearts of the two sisters. They had known loss intimately, having lost their parents to the relentless grasp of the COVID-19 pandemic.

Revanna, at 18, was the elder of the two. She possessed a quiet strength, her gaze steady even in the face of adversity. Rihaana, just 16, carried herself with a grace that belied her youth, her eyes harbouring a depth beyond her years. Together, they went through the unfamiliar terrain of grief and responsibility, their bond forged in the crucible of loss.

In the days following their parents' passing, the sisters found solace in each other's presence. They cocooned themselves within the walls of their home, seeking refuge from the outside world that seemed to move on without them. Together, they cooked meals, tended to household chores, and shared memories of happier times

Revanna sat at the small desk in her cramped bedroom, surrounded by textbooks and notes that had become both her sanctuary and her prison. The immense burden of her decision hung heavy in the air as she stared at the open laptop before her, the glow of the screen casting shadows across her weary face. It was a decision born of necessity; a sacrifice made in the name of survival.

The mortgage payments loomed large, reminding the depth of their precarious situation. And so, with a heavy heart, Revanna made the difficult choice to put her studies on hold and seek employment to keep their home.

It was a bitter pill to swallow for the 18-year-old, whose dreams of a brighter future had been put on hold indefinitely. But she knew that there was no other choice, no other path forward that would allow them to hold onto the only asset they had left. And so, with a sense of resignation, she set out into the world in search of a job that would help keep a roof over their heads.

The search was not easy. In a world ravaged by the economic fallout of the pandemic, opportunities were scarce and competition fierce. Revanna spent hours scouring job listings, submitting applications with a sense of desperation that bordered on despair. Rejection became a familiar companion, each refusal a blow to her already fragile sense of self-worth.

But Revanna was nothing if not resilient. With each setback, she dusted herself off and tried again, her determination to face of adversity was incredible. And finally, after weeks of tireless effort, her perseverance paid off. She landed a job at a local grocery store, her duties ranging from stocking shelves to manning the checkout counter.

The work was gruelling, the hours long and the pay meagre. But Revanna refused to complain, knowing that every penny earned was a step closer to securing their home. She threw herself into her work with a single-minded focus, her studies relegated to the back burner as she juggled the demands of her job with the responsibilities of running a household.

Rihaana always stood by her side, offering words of encouragement and support as Revanna faced the treacherous waters of adulthood. Together, they faced each challenge head-on, their bond growing stronger with each obstacle overcome.

As the days turned into weeks and the weeks into months and nearinga year, Revanna found herself growing weary under the burdening responsibilities, there were moments when doubt crept in, when she questioned whether she had made the right choice in sacrificing her studies for the sake of their home. But then she would look into Rihanna's eyes, filled with a fierce determination that mirrored her own, and she knew that she had made the only choice she could.

Their journey was far from over, and the road ahead was fraught with uncertainty. But if they had each other, Revanna knew that they could weather any storm that came their way. And so, with a sense of resolve born of hardship and sacrifice, she forged ahead, her eyes fixed firmly on the horizon as she fought to secure a future for herself and her sister.

Revanna took on the role of protector, her maternal instincts kicking into overdrive as she assumed responsibility for their well-being. She juggled part-time work with her studies, determined to keep their modest home from slipping through their fingers. Rihaana, ever the dreamer, engaged in her art, her sketches and paintings, to keep her inner turmoil calm.

Their nights were filled with whispered conversations, the darkness providing a veil behind which they could share their fears and aspirations.

The absence of their parents left a void that seemed impossible to fill, an ache that lingered long after the tears had dried. They found themselves struggling with questions that had no easy answers, their grief a silent companion in the empty spaces of their home.

As the world outside continued to spin, Revanna and Rihaana stood steadfast in their resolve to forge a new path forward. They were sisters, survivors, warriors. And though the road ahead was fraught with challenges, they knew that if they had each other, they could face whatever lay ahead.

# Chapter 21

# A New Path

In the tranquil suburb of Brooksville, Mrs. Evelyn Carter, a retired schoolteacher with a passion for gardening and reading, enjoyed the peaceful rhythms of her life. The quiet streets and familiar faces of the neighbourhood had always given her a deep sense of belonging. However, one crisp autumn evening, her routine stroll through the neighbourhood took a troubling turn.

As she walked past the old bakery, Mrs. Carter noticed a group of teenagers huddled in the shadows of an alley. They exchanged furtive glances and small packages, their actions clearly suspicious. Mrs. Carter's heart sank as she realized they were engaged in illegal activity—selling stolen goods. The once-familiar faces now seemed tainted by the desperation of their actions.

Her first instinct was to call the police, but she hesitated. She worried that the intervention of law enforcement might push these young lives further into trouble rather than offer them a chance for redemption. Instead, Mrs. Carter resolved to try a different approach.

The following day, Mrs. Carter approached the teenagers with a gentle smile. They looked up at her with wary eyes, clearly uncomfortable with her presence. "Hi there," she began softly, "I saw you all out there last night. I've been thinking... maybe there's a better way for you to find some purpose." Do you know, Mahatma Gandhi once said,

"The best way to find yourself is to lose yourself in the service of others".

The teenagers exchanged puzzled glances, unsure of what to make of her offer. "What do you mean?" one of them asked, his voice tinged with suspicion.

Mrs. Carter took a deep breath and explained her idea. "I've been talking to the local store manager, and he's agreed to let you help with sorting semi-spoiled fruits and vegetables. You'd be paid for your work, and more importantly, you'd be helping to reduce waste and provide food for those in need."

Another teenager, arms crossed defiantly, snorted. "You want us to sort through garbage? Why would we do that?"

Mrs. Carter's smile remained calm. "I understand it might not sound glamorous, but it's a chance to make a real difference. You'd be contributing to something meaningful, and it's a way to earn money honestly. Plus, I'll be there to support you every step of the way."

The group hesitated; their reluctance evident. But the promise of a modest income caught their interest. After some discussion and a few grumbled agreements, they decided to give it a try.

Their first day at the store was less than enthusiastic. The teenagers arrived with sullen expressions, clearly unimpressed by the task at hand. The work was more laborious than they had anticipated, and their initial excitement quickly waned. Mrs. Carter, however, remained patient and encouraging, frequently stopping by to check on their progress.

"Remember," she said one day as they worked, "this isn't just about the money. It's about making a positive impact.

Your efforts are helping to reduce waste and support those who are less fortunate."

Slowly, the teenagers began to see the fruits of their labour. The store's manager, Mr. Thompson, often shared stories about how their work contributed to feeding families in need. The teenagers started to take pride in their task, their attitudes shifting from reluctance to genuine enthusiasm.

As the weeks turned into months, the once-doubtful group became a cohesive team. Their work ethic improved, and they began to envision a future beyond their past mistakes. Mrs. Carter continued to mentor them, teaching them about budgeting and the value of hard work. She introduced them to the principles of minimalist living, emphasizing that true happiness came from meaningful contributions and simple joys.

One evening, as the group gathered after work, one of the teenagers turned to Mrs. Carter and said, "You know, Mrs. Carter, we didn't think we'd ever say this, but we're actually grateful for this job. It's made a difference for us."

Mrs. Carter's eyes sparkled with warmth. "I'm so glad to hear that. Remember, it's never too late to turn things around and find a path that's right for you."

By offering them an alternative path and guiding them with compassion, Mrs. Carter had not only helped steer the teenagers away from a life of crime but had also given them the opportunity to redefine their futures. They were no longer defined by their past mistakes but by their commitment to making a positive impact on their community.

An American author and educator Henry Adams well penned it,

*"A teacher affects eternity; he can never tell where his influence stops."*

www.ingramcontent.com/pod-product-compliance
Lightning Source LLC
Chambersburg PA
CBHW022017150726
47990CB00002B/695